Michelene Wandor is a po... ...ic. She was born in London in 1940, received her BA in English from Newnham College, Cambridge, and her MA in the Sociology of Literature from the University of Essex. From 1971–82 she was Poetry Editor and theatre reviewer for *Time Out* magazine. She has written extensively for theatre and radio; for the latter, plays such as *An Uncommon Love* about Victorian diarists Arthur Munby and Hannah Cullwick, serials of *Kipps* (H. G. Wells) and *The Brothers Karamazov* (Dostoyevsky), dramatisations of Radclyffe Hall's *The Unlit Lamp*, and Mrs Humphry Ward's *Helbeck of Bannisdale*, and features such as *Dust in the Sugar House* (about Antonia White), *The Ultimate Astonisher* (Dorothy Richardson), and *A Consoling Blue* (Jean Rhys). Her publications include *Five Plays*, *Upbeat* and *Gardens of Eden* (poetry), *Understudies* (on theatre and sexual politics), and as editor, *On Gender and Writing* and four anthologies in an annual series of *Plays by Women*. She has two sons and lives in London.

In the seventeen fictions that make up *Guests in the Body* Michelene Wandor employs a marvellous range of voices – the ironic, the matter-of-fact, a sly and exuberant wit, and the quiet dignity of loss – to create an unusual and pleasurable book.

Is not the soul a guest in the body?

Midrash: *Leviticus Rabbah*, 32
(Quoted in *Treasury of Jewish
Quotations* by Leo Rosten,
Bantam, 1977)

GUESTS IN THE BODY

MICHELENE WANDOR

Published by VIRAGO PRESS Limited 1986
41 William IV Street, London WC2N 4DB

Copyright © Michelene Wandor 1986

British Library Cataloguing in Publication Data
Wandor, Michelene
   Guests in the body.
   I. Title
   823'.914[F]   PR6073.A4/

   ISBN 0-86068-711-2
   ISBN 0-86068-716-3 Pbk

Printed in Great Britain
at Anchor Brendon Ltd of Tiptree, Essex

CONTENTS

ACKNOWLEDGEMENTS

Earlier versions of 'Mother's Pride' appeared in *Spare Rib* and *Upbeat* (Journeyman Press); an earlier version of 'Sweet Sixteen' also appeared in *Upbeat*. An earlier version of 'Breaking and Entering' appeared in the *British Alternative Theatre Directory* (John Offord, 1982). 'Whose Greenham' appeared in *Shifra*, summer 1985, and was first performed as a monologue by Miriam Karlin, at the Riverside Studios, London, in January 1984.

One: Mothers, Music and Dybbuks

The Guest in the Body

Do you know what a soul looks like? Have you ever seen one? Your own, that of a stranger? Would you recognise a soul if you saw one?

I have been thinking about this a lot. I may have seen a soul. I am not sure.

There is a problem. On the whole, the soul cleaves so tight to the body, like a line of writing cleaves to the one above it and to the one below. On the whole, the soul sits comfortably in the body, living through its time, fitting into the crook of the elbow as easily as it fits into anything you can see with your eyes. So how, really, could you even begin to know what to look for? If your soul looks like anything, it probably looks like the air held by a gold ring, but a gold ring that is little more than a soft, moving circle, transparent and yielding, there and not there.

Before the souls entered all the bodies, when the night sky was a deep dark strong and yielding blue, then the sound of the air held in a gold ring sounded softly across the world, and all the souls were tuned to the music of the spheres, and all their different notes had a clear pure rounded sound, each soul its own harmony, the words 'pipe'

3

and 'reed' each having too thin and small an idea in them to be any kind of adequate description. The purity of each sound is heard, because there is very little vibration coming off each note. Each note occupies its space neatly, the ripples holding to the inner circumference of the gold ring. In an earthly instrument there would be ripples moving out from the edges of the note, and these ripples could be heard up to a point, but even when they had ceased to be within the scope of the human ear, they would continue, eddying in inaudibility further and further way, producing auras of sound which people could not hear with their conscious ear, but which worried themselves into the atmosphere around them, and because the ears could not welcome the sounds consciously, the sounds themselves became worried, and came to rest outside the earth's atmosphere, unhappy, unappreciated, so that the entire earth was surrounded by layers and layers of dead sound, arcs of dead sound overlapping other arcs of dead sound. And that is why the air that people breathe in the cities is fraught with worry, with anxiety that cannot be heard, which can be sensed but not put into words, but which is all about the sadness of unheard sound.

So it seems to me, in some way I am trying to understand, that the soul has something to do with sound. And so, perhaps, we are wrong in going around *looking* for the soul. We should, perhaps, be listening for it.

A soul that fits, then, is the air held in a gold ring. A soul that fits is the contented sound after it can no longer be heard. A soul that fits is imperceptible and perhaps you can only tell it is there when it makes you smile.

What, then, of the exception? The soul that doesn't fit? The person whose soul has been pushed to one side, whose soul lives in fearful and cramped quarters, because the body has been squatted, because another soul has claimed the edge of the air. This soul has itself come from a body which has not made peace with itself, which has left unfinished business on earth, which has committed guilt, treachery, unkindness, crime, even; and in this case the squatting soul cannot rest, but is doomed to wander the spaces for which we have no real name. And when the squatting soul inhabits a new body, why, then the indigenous soul has to move over, make way for the invader, and in this it has no choice. Now, you may ask: how does the restless soul find the new body to invade, how does it make itself an involuntary guest in the life of someone who, to all intents and purposes, is innocent?

This is the problem for a mother who is dying. A mother, you might say, is all soul. She comforts, she nurtures, she receives and absorbs suffering. She can never become a *tzaddik*, a righteous and all-knowing one, because only a man can be a true *tzaddik*, but a mother can care for, can care about, can soothe and feed, and her soul reaches to the very edges of the gold ring, the air hugs her luminous circumference. So what happens to the mother, who has been invaded by another soul, by a soul which is restless, not yet at rest, which has to return to earth in the body of another, in order to expiate its sins? The mother's own soul has perhaps become unhappy, tortured without knowing why. The mother only knows that she is suffering, that something within her is deeply sad. She is so used to being able to soothe the troubles of those around her that she has neglected her own unhappiness for years, and she has ignored the alien soul which is troubling her own soul.

Now, when the body is tired, she feels something which is quite apart from the pains and tirednesses of the body. The good and nurturing soul is curled in a corner of the gold ring, still and silent, shining less and less. The restless soul, the *dybbuk*, the invader, the uninvited guest in the body, flexes and moves in the space it has established for itself, and it enters the mother's mind, and it is the voice with which she speaks to herself now. And the soul of the mother, which is not really the soul of the mother, but of someone unknown, from another time and place, this not-soul thinks to the mother: no one is going to hold my hand when I die. I lie propped in this white hospital bed, the starched bedclothes pulled smoothly and sharply around me, clean and crisp, my hands outside the sheets, in one of my arms a drip with life-giving liquid which I don't want, the drip heavily bandaged to my arm, with a splint, because my arm kept bleeding when they were trying to force the tube in, so now my arm looks like a strange, pregnant, bandaged wound. An oxygen mask round my mouth and nose to help my increasingly shallow breathing; when they brought me in here my finger-tips were blue, now at least they are a more normal colour, but I don't care any more. I shut my eyes because what is the bloody point, no one listens to me, besides, it takes too much energy to talk, and now I can only hear myself inside my head, and I am too tired and fed up to answer myself or have a conversation with myself. What the fucking hell – excuse me – so I'll die. I'll be shot of this body, that I can't rely on to piss and shit when I tell it to, that isn't digesting properly any more, when did I last enjoy a chocolate eclair, and when you can't enjoy food any more – well. Without the strength to bend over the bathroom sink any more to wash my hair. At least the sore in my heel healed up, at least that isn't giving me pain, but the rest of the body, oh, get rid of it, get rid of it.

Now, I ask you. This isn't a way to die. This can't be a way to die. This way of dying must be because of the invading soul, because the guest in the body will not let the soul that is rightfully there, will not allow it to move from one way of being to another – from life to death.

At the moment I merely present you with this dilemma. There is very much more investigation to be undertaken. There is, for example, an investigation of why this mother should have been chosen. This mother who has done everything a mother should, who did not once neglect her duty, who never put herself first when she was needed by another, who was what we call 'good'. A good mother. And this is very much a dilemma, which we cannot hope to solve fully here, for it takes time and different times.

Here we can only try and ask some of the right questions, and begin to think some of the right thoughts. Another question – but I think you will already have asked yourself this, because it is the most obvious – another question is, who or what or even why, is this invading soul? What were the events which caused this poor soul to be wandering the air, to know that it could find its own salvation only at the expense of another soul? This is a very long process of investigation.

And there is a third question, one that we do not really want to allow ourselves to ask. This question concerns the nature of the mother. For a soul to invade, and to invade successfully, there has to be some chink in the armour, some weak point in the barricades, some – dare I even approach the mention of it – some kind of welcoming. Perhaps this is more of a thought than a question, because I don't think I dare do more than have the thought at this stage. I do not quite dare ask the question. But I know it is a question, which will not go away until some attempt is made to investigate its possible answer. I am not, after all, intending to turn good into bad, to let bitterness and decay take over. At least, I don't think so. But I think the time has come to investigate the nature of the mother.

I have some thoughts on this; or rather, some words which lead to a thought. The words are: memory metaphor   mother. They all begin with the same letter of the alphabet. All the words for mother I know begin with that letter. Except for the word for mother in Hebrew, and that is written, in English, as 'ima'. And those three letters, in English, also begin the word imagery. So between ima and imagery, mama and metaphor, there is a lot to be thought, a lot to be said, something to be asked, and perhaps a little to be answered.

Whose Greenham

There's a knife under my pillow. There's an orange on my bedside table. I'm a very ordinary woman. I've lived my life and brought up my family. I've never got angry. Except sometimes with the children. It's safe to get angry with the children when they're late home in the winter, or when they get their clothes dirty when you've just put them on clean. Everyone expects you to get angry with children. No one gets at you if you get angry with children. Even if you give them a little smack. Just a little smack.

The knife I've had for fifty-two years. My mother-in-law bought it for me. A bread knife. That was my trousseau. A bread knife and two sets of dinner plates. A *milchedicke* set and a *fleischedicke* set. I always kept a kosher kitchen. Well, up to a point I kept a kosher kitchen. You see, you need two sets of dishes – ah, what's the point. This is a *goyische* country, this isn't a place where being kosher matters to anyone, so not being kosher matters even less.

I'll tell you a joke. There were two old men sitting in a cafe, and one orders a glass of tea with lemon, and the other orders just a glass of tea. So the first old man says to the waiter, 'Make sure the glass is clean.' So the waiter goes out and the waiter comes back carrying the tea, and the waiter says, 'Which one of you wanted the clean glass?'

The orange, my daughter brought me. Yesterday. She comes to see me a couple of times in the week maybe, she doesn't even take her coat off, she sits on a chair for maybe a minute or two, then she starts looking around, restless, then she marches round the room, then she looks at her watch, then she pretends she's just noticed the time, then she says in a very loud voice she's got to go, then she kisses the air near my cheek and she goes. Well.

You can't blame her. She hopes I'll die quietly, like I lived quietly. She doesn't like looking me in the eyes. Something about my eyes being a little watery now, something about the angel of death, the *malach ha mavet*, looking out of one eye and maybe Satan looking out of the other, something in my eyes frightens her. Well.

She found me on the floor. On the kitchen floor. They weren't sure, some sort of stroke, something to do with the heart, you'd think with all their machines and lights they could tell, but no, you can't tell how serious it is going to be, we just have to wait and see. Meanwhile, she seems to be paralysed down one side, she can't co-ordinate with the other, she's lost her powers of speech, maybe she doesn't even understand us, she's better off in hospital where she can have every care and attention.

I've always had very strong lungs. A good voice and really strong lungs. So now, when I get really upset or even just a bit fed up, I scream. I haven't forgotten how to scream, they say at least she can scream, and can I scream, I tell you, they can't stop me once I start. I can go on for half an hour, till their faces are white, till their mouths are tight, but they don't dare shout at me because they know I can shout louder than any of them.

My knife is very sharp. I always kept the bread knife very sharp.

My other daughter is in America. She sends me cards. She sends me flowers with Inter-Flora. They make me sneeze. I hate flowers.

9

I've got sores on my back. All over my back. They're spreading round my front. They're not bed sores. It's me. I'm oozing out of my skin. They itch. I scratch and scratch. They say, how can she have scratch marks all over her when she can't move her arms. They put cream on the sores. I scratch it off. I wonder if I smell. I hope I smell. Badly. The cream they put on the sores is very powerful, and in the long run it will probably work. But it makes the skin thinner, and then all of me, all the me you can't see, will come spilling out, all over this nice clean bed.

I was always a very proud housewife. You could eat off my floor, it was so clean. But why should anyone want to eat off a floor, when there's a clean, white tablecloth on the table?

I'll tell you a joke. In a restaurant, so a man wants to know the time, so he calls to a passing waiter and he asks him the time, so the waiter says 'You're not my table.'

I don't miss not being at home. I had enough of it. He didn't let me have the television up loud enough to hear. So who wants to sit watching a television with the sound turned down? Like it would be if I couldn't hear the nurses, if I was struck deaf and blind, like they want me to be. They think I am watching the world with the sound turned down. I'll tell you, my senses have never been so good. I can hear everything. I can see everything. Good, eh?

He comes to see me every day. He sits, looking at me. Sometimes he pats my hand. Then he looks at me again. Sometimes my eyes are open. Sometimes I keep them shut. But I can see him anyway, so what's the difference. My daughter thinks he has – oppressed – me all these years. Long word, ha? It's her word. But what does she know. It takes two to make a – press – and what the hell anyway. After a while you don't remember what you haven't had. You just nod and smile when they say, what clever children, what beautiful grandchildren, what delicious biscuits, a lovely chicken soup, how did you turn the heel on the socks. You enjoy what you enjoy. Not everyone can have what they want. My daughter doesn't believe that. She thinks you should fight for what you want. And look at her. She has lines round her eyes, her hair is going grey, who is going to look after her when she is old. Ah. Forget it.

I can't chew properly so they give me this special liquid diet. It has all vitamins in it. It has invisible vitamins, all jumping up and down to keep me nutritious and healthy and well and strong. They aren't bothering with any therapy yet because I'm still too much of a vegetable and they want to notice a sign of life or will before they try and bring me back to real life. Good, eh? Real life.

I miss the romances a bit. Being a vegetable, of course I can't read. So all the library books are back in the library. My 'rubbish', he calls it. I like Catherine Cookson, and some others, I forget which. Sometimes I like a happy ending and sometimes I like an unhappy ending. It depends.

My daughter, my educated daughter, thinks I waste my time on the books. I made her clothes to go to university with, we worked hard to get her an education, now I educated her so far away from me, we got nothing to talk about. Except the children and how she is and whether she's earning a living, and none of that she wants to talk about. Well, the hell with her. Very simple. She doesn't want to talk, so don't talk. He doesn't want to talk, so don't talk. I'm invisible now so I don't have to talk. I can talk any language I want. English, Yiddish, Hebrew, German, Polish. Right? Any one I like, when I like. I don't care who's listening. I don't care if no one is listening.

When she came yesterday, my daughter couldn't stay because she's going away for a couple of days and she's got a lot to do. To Greenham, she says, she thinks I'm not hearing a word, so she tells me all about it, with her back to me, so I won't hear her and I won't see her lips move, and she says in her words, so she says she's going to Greenham because she believes it is right and time for women to do something about peace. She thinks only women understand what peace is truly about, and only women care about the lives of the unborn, and only women care for there to be a world for the young to grow up in, and now she really understands what politics means and she's going to sleep under a piece of plastic and she shall not be moved and her spirit will go on and on. She thinks she knows it all. She thinks she knows what everyone in the world is thinking. Well, she says, if you – meaning me – was well, you could come with me, there are a lot of older women down there, women of all ages. She knows her mother so well, she thinks I will sleep in the mud under a piece of plastic. Of course I don't say anything. But I think of my knife. Under my pillow.

So she takes the orange out of her coat pocket and she puts it on the bedside table and then she tells me how last week all the women lined up at the wire and they pulled and pushed and they got the wire down from the fence, where it is, round the missile base, and she says on the other side was a young soldier, just about the same age as her son, she has a son of twenty, so this young soldier he hit at her knuckles and he made them bleed, and she looked at him, and there was hatred in his eyes and there was hatred in her eyes. She says to me, my daughter, her hand still on the orange, she says to me, straight to me, facing me, so I could see her lips move in case I'm deaf, she says with approval, she says they faced one another with hate. This makes her happy. This she likes. This is her idea of being angry. Hate makes her happy. She doesn't want to argue, she just wants to hate. Well.

My daughter thinks she is doing the right thing. My daughter is sure she is doing the right thing. I can see in her eyes she is already somewhere else, she is thinking she doesn't want to be here with a mother like a vegetable, that although she can hate the soldier, she cannot allow herself to hate me because she is afraid of me. And she is more afraid of being afraid of me than she is of these guns, or whatever they are. I don't care whatever they are.

I'll tell you a joke. Hitler is feeling a little insecure, so he calls up a fortune teller and he asks the fortune teller what is in store for him. So the fortune teller tells him he, Hitler, will die on a Jewish holiday. So Hitler asks, which particular holiday is that going to be, so the fortune teller says to Hitler, 'Any day you die will be a Jewish holiday.' Well. You can imagine what happened to the fortune teller.

She begins to peel the orange, so that the rind is in one long, delicate spiral.

I can't move. I can't walk. I can't speak. I can't hear. I can't cook dinner. I can't do the washing. I can't do the shopping. I can't hoover. I can't wash the floor. I've never been happier in my life. I got it all worked out. I can't move, so I can't peel an orange. I can't move, so I couldn't have put the knife into my handbag while my daughter tele-phoned for the ambulance. I can't move, so I couldn't have kept the knife under the mattress, which they never turn. I can't move, so I couldn't have taken the knife out from under the mattress and put it under my pillow. So.

The next person who comes into this room I'm going to kill. I don't mind who it is. I'm not fussy. It may be my daughter. It may be my husband. It may be a nurse or the lady with the tea that I never drink. I don't care. No one will know. On this knife, which I didn't wash very often, who needs to wash a bread knife often, on this knife, there are my finger-prints, my daughter's finger-prints and my husband's finger-prints. My finger-prints, who's going to notice, a vegetable can't kill, a potato doesn't rise up and fight back. So.

You want to know exactly how? I'll tell you. You take the knife – so. You put the tip of it against the person's heart, so. Or you could put it against their back, I suppose, but I can't show you that. So against the heart. Then you press it in, very quick and sudden – you don't want anything to go wrong at the last moment – so.

She dies.

If you're lucky, there's even no blood. They keep the sheets lovely and white here.

It is the forgèd feature finds me; it is the rehearsal
Of own, of abrupt self there so thrusts on, so throngs the ear.

Henry Purcell by Gerard Manley Hopkins
(OUP, 1956)

Sex According to Vivaldi
(*or* The Danger of Angels)

When the sun strikes the water, on a clear, clean day, you can see sudden light; sudden flashes of light. Flashes of light which you can hear. The flash of an octave, one note answering, echoing the other, from a higher, playful place, a spark of recognition flashing between the two. You can see figures of light, pyramids and hills and columns of arpeggios and chords, you can see semi-quavers rippling out from the octave, you can see light flashing in intervals of a dazzling second, a minor third, a perfect fifth.

Antonio used to say that if there really was a God, then God must have invented the octave, by seeing what happened when the sun struck the water and was reflected back unto itself. That would be on the fourth day of Creation, when the sun and moon were created. The ripples, the waves sent out by the water, flashing in sparks and semi-circles of light, the ripples must be the scales and arpeggios, pursuing the same sequence of patterns, over and over again, different combinations, different permutations, and isn't it all beautiful?

If I believe in God – and I'm not at all sure that I do – but if there is a God and a heaven, then I imagine its streets will be paved with water and music will rise like steam in the sunlight. Like Venice. The Venice of marble and water, voices and music.

Antonio is crying. Deep, wracking sobs. In bed. We are making love for the very first time and he is crying. Why? It's all wrong. It's the woman who is supposed to be overcome with sadness. It's the woman who is supposed to be shattered at the loss of something or other, some non-existent innocence, at a moment of transition. Here we are, holding each other, and he is crying. What have I done? How dare you? What's wrong? Is it me? Is it us? Is it – the impossibility of it all? A word – a sob – a sentence – and then words, words, tumbling out, laughing – all these months and us pretending that what passes between us is merely music, all these months, and I sit in the orchestra and watch you as I play or as I sing and I think that you are merely my conductor, and I am merely a musician, and that you only look at me as you would look at any other musician. And there, behind every accidental, every syncopated phrase, we have been touching, and touching each other, always, touching each other so naturally that it seems almost unimportant. And look at us now. Crying and laughing, moving in a quiet pulse and slipping into sleep together.

When we give concerts in the Pietà, there was always a metal grille between us and our audience. It was considered improper for the secular gentlemen in the chapel to catch even the slightest glimpse of one of the young girls. It was, however, considered perfectly proper for them to listen to us play and sing. How strange. I can think of nothing more likely to inflame the imagination of young men and women than the most beautiful music in the world, performed by invisible voices. The danger of angels is as nothing to the music we made.

I remember one concert. Through the bars of the grille I can see a man's hand, tapping, tap-tapping on his knee. A grey, woollen knee. I think he's enjoying the music, I suppose he must be enjoying the music, and he thinks he's tapping his hand in time to the music. Tap – tap – tap tap . . . tap . . . but he hasn't, he doesn't, he can't hear where one beat ends and another begins, he can't hear how one line plays with another – tap tap tap – I can't take my eyes off him – tap tap tap tap tap – out of the corner of my eye I can see the thin iron bars, a little chipped and flaking tap tap   hard and chipped and flaking   tap   and then the fingers, soft white, fat   tap tap tap   refined tap tap   beating and beating some rhythm that refuses to allow any other rhythm and it is squeezing its way through the bars and into my head and my brain and around me I can feel the pulse of the music and in my head I can feel the wrongness tap tap tapping its way through my eyes into my brain – oh, it is the devil, I am in the presence of the devil and he will destroy me, he will draw me into his dark pulse-less world with his fingers – and then – two bars before my entry in the Largo – somehow I drag my eyes away from his fingers. I have been in deadly combat with the devil, and I have won.

After the concert, Antonio congratulated me on my performance. I had been exemplary, he said, in the intensity of my concentration. That night we made love for the first time.

From this window, I can see the outer wall of the orphanage. Down there, just by the hospital wing, there is a part of the wall which has an iron grate set into it, low down in the stone, reaching to the ground. Between the edge of the grate and the paving stone underneath, there is a sort of smooth, curved hollow in the stone. There is just enough room to lay a new-born baby in this stone hollow, so that it can be slipped under the grate, to the other side of the wall, into the cloister. Every morning one of the Sisters used to go down to the grate, to see if a baby had been left there. Sometimes you could hear the baby crying. The babies were taken in and looked after in the hospital wing, on the far side, so that their crying shouldn't disturb the older girls, I suppose. No one ever knew where the babies came from. No one asked. The children of poor and devout people, perhaps, the children of prostitutes, foundlings, love-children. Odd, the phrase, 'love child'.

I was fourteen when I arrived here. Fourteen and furious. Betrothed at fourteen, not delighted about it, like my friend Isabella, oh no, not collecting pairs of shoes in anticipation of my marriage, like Isabella, oh no, one for each year of her life, fourteen pairs, decorated with gold and silver lace, with tiny blue flowers and scarlet bows. Not delicate and good and obedient and always pretty and smiling, like Isabella, not liking the young man chosen to be my husband, chosen for me by my father when we were still babies, a convenient arrangement between fellow bankers, and a glass of Chianti to celebrate. I won't look at a dull spotty boy; I won't acknowledge his presence. I don't want to know him and I will not marry someone I don't know. Kicking and screaming and tears and tantrums and here I am, thrown into prison, to learn, says my father, the meaning of devotion and obedience, to come to my senses.

I came to my senses.

If you walk through Venice on a summer night, past the open windows, the candles, the light, the music, everyone is singing and playing and dancing in the palaces. I could play the violin when I came here. I could play the notes, that is. Not the music. Here I had no choice. Music all the time. I liked the speed of sound under my fingers. Antonio wrote for me. People called me a virtuoso. People called him a virtuoso. It isn't a word I understand. The sound comes from deep within you, it is your own being speaking through your fingers. The first time I heard Antonio play I recognised something. And I knew that I was not in prison. I had been set free from prison. I had come to my senses.

People nicknamed Antonio 'the Red Priest'. His hair, of course, but also his incredible passions. I used to hold my arm under his head at night, for fear the heat of his hair, the dark and flame and burning colour, might burn the

17

pillow, might singe the initials I had so carefully embroidered on the fine linen.

Antonio does not really want to become a priest. He wants to play music. He wants to play his violin. He has a million sounds in his head. He must write them down. His father tells him that he will find it easier to earn his living as a musician if he becomes a priest. That way he will find an automatic place in the social order. Writing music is, after all, part of the duties of a priest who plays to celebrate the Divine Spirit.

He takes Holy Orders. He takes Mass for a year. He has to raise his voice in the Mass. When he sings with his own human voice, he breathes in and in, he doesn't seem to have enough air for the long phrases, he gasps and gasps and an iron band comes down across his head, over his eyes, and another heavy iron band closes itself around his chest and his mouth is open and gasping in and he cannot let go so that the air and the music can come out, and his arms fall to his side and his shoulders hunch and he staggers away from the altar and into the dark and the silence and the cool of the sacristy and he falls onto a wooden bench and supports the intolerance of his heavy body on his hands as gradually his shoulders fall and his jaw relaxes and the iron band releases itself and in the quiet he lets the air flow out of him and away and the roaring in his ears settles and in its place comes a melody, a chord, notes running freely, and he finds the quill and a piece of paper and he writes and writes until the music is caught and resting in black and white. Antonio no longer takes Mass. But it is too late to halt the rumour that he is careless of his religious duties.

Of course Antonio's father was right. How else, but as a priest, could he have such opportunities for music. How else, but as a priest, could he have come to work in the Pietà, among the nuns and the girls, how else would I have met him, how else made music for him, how else would he have given me music.

At the back of the building, jutting onto a small canal, dark, where no sunlight can creep into the crevices, there are the store-rooms. There the silence is dark, and haunts the ears.

Me. Huge, like a whale, beached. Sister Teresa, a pink oleander flower in her hair. I am in pain. I am in agony. I shatter the silence. I sip wine and water between my agonies.

Antonio, sitting in the corner, hunched, among the oranges, the smoked hams, the onions and the garlic. His red hair glowing. As I groan and try not to make too much noise, I can see his head turning, to and fro, as it does when his body sways to the movements of his arms playing the violin, to and fro, and a sharp pain builds in me and I cry out and he leaps up and runs, runs out of the room, away, away, and the pain suddenly stops short, cut off by his going and instead I cry because he has abandoned me in my great need. Teresa holds me as I sob, and wipes my forehead, and kisses me and strokes my hair and holds me as the next pain touches me in my centre and tells me it is coming again.

And I open my mouth to let the pain out, and there is a sound of great and true beauty, and it replaces the sound I would have made, and Antonio is in the room, by my side, he and his violin improvising to my rhythms, to the sway and swell of the stardust in the room, and the harvest of food in the corner, and the scent of oranges and onions and the thick white wax of the candles, and my body follows a music I learned somewhere else, and we learn together, first the three of us, and then the fourth, Anna, our daughter. And her music takes over from ours, and she sucks at my breast straight away and we are all silent together.

Teresa told the other nuns that she had found the baby that morning, in the hollow stone, under the grate in the wall. We had no choice. Some other women also have no choice, and they wrap their babies tightly and throw them, weighted with stones, into the dank, backstreet canals of the city.

I want to try and say something about – I want to try and

— to say — about something that — you see, I have — I have been — I am — this —

Antonio in rehearsal, shouts, is sarcastic, is loud and angry, is cold and sarcastic, can't you hear, can't you land on the notes in their centre, I want perfection and you will give it to me as if I were giving it to myself. In private I shout at him, you are an arrogant bastard, you know you can't have perfection without imperfection, you know that perfect pitch and perfect harmony only exist in relation to imperfect harmony and discord, and what is this stupid word perfection, anyway? Who are you to tell me what is pure, who are you to want purity and perfection all the time, don't you know that you only want the pure because you know it is possible to misread a note, to know that timing can be wrong, that one person is capable of not listening to another, that good intentions are not enough, it is something relative. No, no, no. His face fiery red, his nails, bitten down to the quick, flat against the tips of his white fingers, no, no, no, don't you see, the whole point, the whole struggle is against inaccuracy, against imperfection, the whole point is to be absolutely in the right place at the right time. No, no, no. I don't want to hear about the right place at the right time, I don't want to hear about perfect pitch, I don't want to hear about infallible timing. I see my daughter at a distance, I watch her laugh, I hear her play and sing, and I say nothing to her and she doesn't know who I am, and I have not sung or played a note since she was born and who dares talk to me about the right place at the right time.

Antonio and I did not make love again after Anna was born. We loved, as ever, with complete devotion, we slept in the same bed. But we never touched in the same way.

Antonio was a brilliant teacher. Coaxing, cajoling, bullying, threatening, praising; sarcastic and brutal. Gentle and enabling.

After Anna was born, I had a great desire to leave the Pietà. But where would I have gone? I did not want to leave Antonio. I did not want to be out of sight of my daughter.

At night I sneaked out sometimes. Wearing a dark cloak, carrying a basket, so that people in the streets think I'm a maid hurrying home from work, a nurse hurrying to tend the sick, a whore hurrying to a rendezvous. I wander for hours sometimes, in the silence of sewage and the lives which shout down from the windows in the back streets. I make the journey between silence and music regularly, outside the stone walls which contain me during the day.

Antonio finally left Venice for good. We had always travelled a lot, all over Europe, and particularly to Amsterdam, to talk business with his music publisher there. Dutch music printing was far in advance of its Venetian counterpart, a clearer script, much more suitable for the shapes of Antonio's music. Antonio was older, perhaps a little tired of Venice's insatiable demands for new music, going out of fashion, perhaps, in favour of newer composers. I went with him, part of the entourage. I nursed him when he was ill. I wrote the music for him when he was tired. Often I knew what was in his mind, and would finish something he had started.

Sign my name to it? Of course not. It isn't my music. All right, maybe some of it is my music, but how do I know what is mine and what is yours, and don't shout at me, you know it brings on your asthma. I will not sign my damn name, damn you, I will not take over where you left off, this is not my music, it is your music and I would not be writing if it were not for you. I will not play my violin, I will not go away and compose something and play it to you, who is going to listen to anything an unknown woman will compose, where are the women priests who are the *maestri di coro*, who are the *maestri di musica*, need I bloody go on. He is silent. No, he says, very calmly. Don't go on. Just sing to me, play to me, as you used to. I swear at him, and run out of the room, so that he should not see my tears.

Antonio died last year. Somewhere unknown. Buried somewhere, in a pauper's grave, with no name on it.

I have not seen Venice for seven years. Water on stone; the caged nightingales singing in the little shops by the bridges, the wax candles in the cathedrals, building marble shadows.

It was raining when Antonio was buried. The rain drifted through my head, sinking into the earth. A funeral hymn, soft and light, not at all sacred, water on earth on stone. I have played the music in my head all through the long solitary journey back here to the Pietà. In my old room I have written the melody. In my old room I have brought my music to life. I am singing it to myself.

Anna is fourteen.

She is very dark, like me; she has a patrician nose, with a sort of bump in the middle, a wonderfully arrogant profile. She pitches herself perfectly into incessant activity; never still. She is the most beautiful thing in Venice. They tell her she is a virtuoso. She laughs at them. She laughs and laughs, in a fiery sort of way, and she sings and plays and laughs with a voice I have carried inside me. I am going to tell her who she is.

Antonio left no will.

Mother's Pride

No one knew who she was at first. There was no identification in the car; she hadn't taken her bag, no money, nothing. It took a while to trace the children. They were staying with her parents for the weekend.

I often get absent-minded when the children are away. It's as though I'm suddenly able to see a long way, like when you go into the country and the horizon is miles away and your eyes hurt, trying to look that far. A sort of vertigo.

I also get really sloppy when the kids are away. Once I was cleaning up their room and I found a pair of smelly socks, tucked away in the corner behind one of the bunk beds. I started crying, just like that, for no reason. I suppose things like that make me look forward to when they'll be back, so I can nag them to put their dirty clothes in the washing bag, and who do they think I am, someone who's got nothing better to do than run around after them, clearing up, am I your *slave* or something? No, Mum, just my mother and where did you put my clean football socks?

I didn't want another child. Three's enough, especially after managing on my own all those years. Well, mainly on

23

my own, I met him a couple of years after my husband died. But I still think of it as 'being on my own'. Not that you're ever on your own with three noisy kids.

It would have been due sometime in late September. It must have happened the night we hung around in the Kingfisher's Arms, well after closing time, and the landlady shooed us out, reminding us that she still had all the glasses to wash up and be up at seven the next morning for a delivery of Guinness. That must have been the Monday after my last period finished, no, Doctor, I can't remember the exact date it started, well, no, I don't write it down, I am a woman of today, I just go with the flow. I don't like to think that science can fail me, and anyway, I don't connect sex and fertility unless I decide to. If men don't, why should I?

Of course I had my diaphragm in, would I lie to you, Doctor, I always put it in, well, after eight years on the pill, I'd had enough, and have you heard the one about the doctor who tells this woman who got pregnant on the cap that she should have been on the pill and she says, I tried that, Doctor, but it kept falling out.

He loves my children. It took him a while to get round to it but he loves them. He's like most people really, he'd rather have his own. You want to see what it looks like, don't you, whether two people can really reproduce another whole human being, all your own work, all there, in every detail. Of course you don't *both* produce it in the same way. I always think of the children as 'mine', even though I am fully aware of the scientific facts of the case. Some people are romantic to the verge of mysticism about their children, and I suppose if you are religious, then you probably believe the whole thing is a gift from God. Other people think of it as the division of labour; I've always thought that was a bit ironic, given that it's the woman who has to go through labour.

He's never tried to persuade me to have his child. He'd be really pleased if I wanted another child, but he's never tried to put pressure on me. You'd think that knowing it would be my decision would make it easier for me to choose, you know, my body, my choice.

It's funny that thing about choice. I mean, some women can decide to have a child on their own; it's hard, but I know someone who did it. She'd been living alone since she left school, and she was getting into her thirties, and she thought, well, it's now or never, so she decided, right, it's now. So, nine months later, after an obliging friend obliged . . . Now a man can't do that, can he. He has to find a woman who will have the baby, however much he may really want to be a father.

The truth is I don't want to have to choose. It gives me vertigo. Green hills so far away, you can't quite make them out. Like most other women, I've never trusted men with taking precautions. I was prepared to make all the choices about contraception, but I got so fed up. Sun-yellow pill? Pretty pale rubber cap? Wiggly little coil? Side-effects. I read somewhere that the most commonly used contraceptive is the sheath, but I would never trust them; anyway, the sort of men I like are all quite well-educated and none of them seem at all keen on the sheath. Must be something to do with them being so articulate. They can talk their way out of anything.

I don't think men really understand how much energy women expend on worrying about these things. I don't suppose they can; for some reason they find it hard to imagine. I suppose they get near it if they're there when their baby is being born. But more ordinary things – like, say, having a period. Stupid word, that. Period. In America it means 'full stop', like in punctuation. That's stupid as well. A period isn't a full stop. It's a new beginning. I don't mean all that creativity, life-giving force, earth-mother stuff, I mean it's a new beginning to the month, relief that you're not pregnant, when you don't want to have a child. Unless, of course, you want to be pregnant, and then a period is a momentary full stop to the wanting, a disappointment – oh, I suppose period isn't such a bad word. It's better than the curse. Being on the rag.

If I got pregnant and decided to have an abortion, he would back me up, take me to the hospital, bring me home. He would understand, he would be disappointed, but he would understand. I would have no difficulty getting an abortion on the National Health. I didn't last time. Widow, three children, the youngest only two? The consultant couldn't refuse me. He believed in a woman's right to choose, he granted me my abortion, then he lectured me and said a woman of my age couldn't afford to get pregnant by accident and I was to go on the pill when it was all over, and I was scared he'd take my abortion away like it was my Sunday ice-cream and I very humbly thanked him for making the decision for me.

She was neatly dressed, her insurance and driving licence quite up-to-date; the car tyres were in perfect condition, the steering and brakes excellent.

I remember lying on the trolley just outside the operating theatre, two large men in green wheeled me up there, my Green Cross Code men, I thought. I didn't have a pillow under my head and I was vaguely dopey from the pre-med injection and I must have been whimpering a bit with fear, like children do when they're asleep and one of the green men said to me: 'Don't be silly, you've had three children, you know what it's all about.' He must have read my notes. Even I hadn't read my notes. He was a green monster who wanted me to behave like a mother even though I was about to unbecome the possibility of being one. Someone in white came along with another needle and I thought, the hell with you, if I want to have a little whimper, I bloody well will. And I did. Then the next second – jab.

I told him later that it was like being switched off like an electric light. That's what dying must be like, I said, just being switched off.

The medical reports say that she was in the early stages of pregnancy, about six to eight weeks.

I try to imagine what it would be like, having a tiny baby again. Obsessed with every moment of its bodily ins and outs, holding its face against mine, feeling its tiny breath moving against my cheek. I don't think I want to get heavier and heavier, have to pee every five minutes, have to rest my legs when they ache, feel someone is feeding off me inside, growing and kicking, warm and loving, taking me over, depending on me, stealing the calcium from my bones and teeth, the iron from my blood at night, promising to love me and trust me and depend on me.

On Saturday I did all the shopping for a week. My father came to collect the kids in a flurry of coats and wellies, to stay with them on the farm. I cleaned the house and then I went for a drive round London, past all the green places where people were walking, picnicking in the sun. I looked at the tiny babies, asleep in their carry-cots, on their stomachs, the backs of their heads bald from where their hair had rubbed away when they lay on their backs. I saw babies of a few months old propped up, trying to hold onto their bottles. I watched toddlers running around in the grass, falling over and bouncing up again. Bits of rusk in the prams, bare legs with little rolls of fat above the knee.

On Sunday I did the washing, in the washing machine I'd finally managed to save up for. That would make washing nappies a pushover. Well, a rinse-over. I hadn't had a washing machine with the other three. Or a car. All that came slowly, earning and saving. I knew I could take time off my job – ten years ago I'd never even heard of maternity leave. The older children would babysit, they might even like the idea. When the other three flew the nest, I would still have someone to love me and depend on for my old age, whether he was still around or not. You can never love anyone the way you love your children, can you?

I drove around a lot that weekend. I would plan the abortion, organise my timetable to take a couple of days off work, then I would see a warm laughing baby and cry. I would plan the birth, the excitement of doing it right and shared and happy. Then I would see a woman, her hair scrunched back behind her ears with that haunted hectic look peculiar to mothers of toddlers; and I would cry.

On Sunday afternoon I was on my way home, and I stopped at these traffic lights. In front of me was another car. We were both in the right-hand lane, and in the left-hand lane there was an articulated lorry. The lights changed and I changed into first gear. Then everything happened very quickly. The lorry seemed to jack-knife to the right, I tried to speed up to get past him, he seemed to change direction as if he was trying to avoid me, I skidded, tried frantically to remember which way to turn the wheel, and just before everything switched off, I remember seeing that the lorry had a sticker on the windscreen saying 'Cheer up, the Tories are coming', and a van drove past at great speed to avoid the crunch, and on the side of the van it said 'Mother's Pride'. Neat, that.

Death was instantaneous. She must have gone out like a light.

The shock must have brought on my period. I must say it was a relief. I've got to go back to the hospital next week to have the plaster taken off my arm. I heard that the woman driving the other car was killed. I don't know anything about her. I wonder if she had trouble making decisions.

Lullaby

A dog is barking. A high-pitched, insistent, nervous bark, repeating and repeating. She sits up in bed. The house is quiet, except for the soft, purring tick of the bedside clock. The curtains are partly drawn back. Outside there is a cold moon light.

The sheets are a deep royal blue, like the sky. A small black fly lands on the back of her right hand. She watches its legs, fine black hairlines against the skin's pallor. The fly walks across the back of her hand, raising the hairs on her hand as it moves. She slaps it hard with the palm of her left hand. Another fly lands on her right hand. She slaps it again. She pulls back the rumpled sheet. A scurry of black flies leap and flutter in dismay. She tries to slap them flat on the bed but there are too many. She pulls the sheet back further, slowly and carefully, and there is a swirl of lighter, worm-coloured creatures. Somehow she knows that they are a larva-form of the black flies. She watches them squirm and squiggle over and around each other, like maggots in a fisherman's tin.

She lifts a hand to – sweep them wriggling onto the floor? smash them into the sheet? Her hand is suspended, and paralysed, she watches the worms at the edge of the eddying shape grow fatter, hair begins to sprout from their wriggling bodies, they are taking up more and more room in the bed, like gigantic caterpillars. The sheet is black with their bodies, a live, moving sea. She slowly stands up, praying that none of the creatures has left its mark on her.

She goes downstairs.

A dog is barking somewhere outside.

She makes a cup of tea. She sits down at the kitchen table.

A dog is barking. The sound is very close.

Her hand knocks the cup of tea in alarm. It spills. In slow motion a chocolate-coloured waterfall leaps over the edge of the mug, splaying onto the formica table-top.

She hears snuffling. She goes to the kitchen door and looks into the hall. The front door is slightly ajar. Standing on the doorstep, its front feet already on the hall carpet, is a small black and white dog. It is worrying at a piece of mouldy meat, covered with bits of fluff. It begins to bark, then seizes the piece of meat, throws it up into the air, drops it again and is about to bite at the meat when it utters a sharp yelp, spins round in a circle and sits doubled up, one back leg stuck straight up in the air, as its mouth burrows at its flea-bitten soft centre.

She stays where she is, and says 'shoo' softly. The sound has the opposite effect. The dog looks up and runs past her into the kitchen.

She turns back into the kitchen. The sink is full of brown tin plates smeared with dried food. On the draining board are two porridge-lined saucepans, their contents dry, browning and cracked.

The window sill is crammed with milk bottles, many partly full of sour and souring milk, some with mould round the rims, others empty, but with cloudy cheesy rims round them. The dog is now playing with a ball of bright green wool, dulled where it is covered in clouds of dust which flail out into the air as the dog barks and attacks it. The dog bites its own fur as it gets wrapped in the unravelling wool, emitting little yelps of anger or irritation or pleasure – she can't tell.

The cookery books are cascaded all over the room, mixed up with old bits of greasy newspaper, sticky with deposits of various kinds, some books with pages ripped out, some with burned covers, curled up at the edges.

The dog grabs at one of the books, worrying and chewing at it, then it suddenly dives at her feet, yapping at her toes, biting at them. She kicks out wildly and hears the dull thud of foot on crunching bone and the dog's yelps rise an octave to a continual high-pitched screaming, its tail whips between its legs and it runs out and away into the deserted night street.

She goes back to the table, to finish her tea. The mug is empty. The inside is lined with brown rings, merging at the bottom of the cup into a continuous brown, tannin layer. Black flies are crawling over the table, drinking from the spilled puddle of tea. She stretches her hand out to wave the flies away and a cloud of them rises up. She snatches her hand back and stands there, shoulders hunched, hands clasped together. Her nightdress feels dry, flaky, it is crumbling under her fingers, turning into flaked pieces of old paper. The dust seeps into her veins. Her hands are crawling with mites and lice, her skin is fermenting with yeasts. Her hair tickles her scalp, hundreds of tiny spiders are weaving webs around her eyes, tightening their hold until she cannot move her head at all. Her nails are grey with dust, it is entering her eyes, her ears.

The front door bangs hard. She shivers. The sound of footsteps along the hall, the kitchen door opens. What on earth is going on, he says. She looks down at her hand, holding a squeaking clean, shining milk bottle. The milkman, she said, I forgot to put the bottles out for the milkman. Come back to bed, he says, reaching out his hand for hers – come on, you must be freezing down here. I'll just put this bottle outside, she says, lifting it up to examine it against the light, to check whether it is clean. I might as well make a cup of tea, he says, now we're both up. Yes, she says, that would be nice. Be careful, he says, you're dripping water onto the floor.

Oh, that doesn't matter, she says, some people are much messier than me.

Sweet Sixteen

Sixteen soft pink blankets fold inwards over sixteen soft warm smiling babies. Sixteen dark-haired young mothers meet their sixteen babies' soft smiling mouths in a kiss. Sixteen mothers and babies recede into the soft-focus blues and greens of sixteen immaculate gardens.

Naomi looks round to see the cluster of other mothers, like herself, mesmerised by Granada TV Rental's windows. The mothers swap little grins and turn their attention back to the real babies bundled in push-chairs and prams. The cluster breaks, and its various components span out across the cool marble floor, past the glass and perspex walls, through the chrome and glass doors and into the world of echoing footsteps, surrounding arcades and fountains and climbing and weeping shrubbery.

Lucy strains to stand up in her push-chair. Naomi eases her out of the canvas straps and settles her on the red seat of the silver trolley. She pauses momentarily, to decide which is to be the first aisle of the journey; should she start with soft drinks, vegetables, frozen foods, tins – she decides on fruit juice. As they wheel past the rack of special-offer

Mars bars, Naomi gently deflects Lucy's outstretched hand, her thumb briefly stroking the soft palm of Lucy's hand. I could do the shopping with my eyes shut, thinks Naomi, once a week for how many weeks, everything always in the same place. She turns the trolley to the right, to the fridge where the pineapple juice cartons – she stops. The open maw of the fridge gapes. It is empty. Ah well. Perhaps they have run out of cartons of fruit juice.

She decides to do dairy products next; cream, butter, some yoghourt – but instead, on the racks where the dairy products used to be, she finds pizzas, steak and kidney pies in coy transparent wrappings, and further on packets of frozen, sleeping raspberries and apple and blackberry crumbles. Something is wrong. She begins to collect, feeling uneasy that it isn't in the order of her choice, worried that if she leaves things now to go on to another aisle, they will have disappeared when she gets back.

She wheels on, to where she expects to find the vegetable racks: the net bags of French apples, the South African avocados, severely boycotted each time. But instead there are long blue and red spaghetti packets, rice, curled dusty pasta. Again she collects, panic beginning to rise. She mustn't show it to Lucy, who is happy being wheeled at such sight-seeing speed, happy to have her outstretched hand denied, because her desire is being stroked at the rate of new products every thirty seconds.

Naomi makes confidently for the cold meat counter; it is dark, piled up with unattended towers of soft toilet paper; the plastic box where scraps of meat were sold cheaply, the ends of cuts, is upside down, empty. For the first time she notices the other women. They walk fast, their heads slightly bent, cradling high-piled baskets, anxiety on their faces, grabbing cereals, bread, soap powders, cleansers, hurrying past pensioners, skirting toddlers, running, running.

Lucy now has a fist in her mouth, enjoying the game, enjoying the deftness of the domestic dodgems where years of unthinking practice has enabled the women to anticipate corners, come to a full stop at the precise point of need, to turn in a tight space, to avoid and yet not slacken speed. Naomi speeds up to join the pace, taking what she can wherever she can, until she arrives at the back of the floor space, at the point where the soft drinks used to be. Naomi gasps. The once smooth space is now a raw gash, copper cables twisting like thick muscle fibre, clinging to the broken brick and plaster gaps in the walls.

Naomi hears a voice saying, Nothing is where it was. Lucy giggles and she realises that she has spoken out loud. She looks round. No one seems to have heard her. They are all too busy. Naomi looks down at the trolley. It is full of everything she has meant to buy, but none of it is in the right order, the order she is used to.

Naomi wheels the trolley slowly towards the cash tills. Lucy, sensitive to the change in pace, stops giggling; she is now pale and still. Naomi joins a queue at a cash till, watching the other women, their eyes darting, their hands cupped protectively over their prospective purchases, as if there were some danger of someone whisking everything out again and back onto the alien shelves.

Naomi stands behind a woman who fumbles for her cheque book. Naomi watches as the white snakes with purple figures spill out of the tills, paper bags, plastic carriers, boxes and baskets flash between the tills and the plate glass window.

Naomi's turn comes. She lifts a bottle of lemon and lime out of the trolley. The outside is sticky. Naomi moves her index and second fingers to a dry part of the bottle, her hand slips, the bottle falls, its soft edge knocks against the rim of the conveyor belt and bursts.

Thick, bright green liquid squirts luminously back into the trolley, over tins of tuna fish. Lucy claps her hands in delight, and reaching into the trolley, she lifts a packet of white self-raising flour and drops it with a dull thud on the floor. A white cloud powders the feet of the women. Lucy giggles. Naomi feels a cloud of answering laughter rise in her, tries to keep it down, looks up and catches the eye of the woman queuing behind her. The woman smiles, ruffles

Lucy's hair and then lifts a bag of tomatoes from her own basket and hurls it overarm against the special offer of tea bags. Red seed drips down against the green boxes.

The women look at one other. Suddenly bits of flattened, squared ham fly free of their jellied, cellophane packets, duck pâté bursts out of its blue pottery bowls, salt and vinegar crisps crackle underfoot, sliding through whiter than white cottage cheese, a treacle pudding roosts among the spilled biscuit crumbs. The air is thick with suspended golden arcs from tinned peaches, rains of mint-flavoured petit pois, chunky Branston pickle washed along by mineral water from Malvern spa.

The lights of the cash tills spark white, the women sitting at the money machines aren't sure which way to turn, one surreptitiously picks up a cucumber and slides it along the floor, into a welcoming pool of raspberry yoghourt.

Outside the plate glass window red and blue lights flash as pale men in dark blue peer through the window at all the Christmas and birthday and anniversary celebrations in one.

Ten feet away, sixteen dark-haired mothers smile at their babies for the sixteenth time and enfold them in sixteen warm, pink blankets.

I am the Kind of
Woman Who

I am the kind of woman who.

I am the kind of woman who lives in a place that is sometimes a castle and sometimes a ghetto.

I am the kind of woman who needs central heating.

I am the kind of woman who gives way to other people on the pavement.

I am the kind of woman who always moves her umbrella aside to avoid knocking into the umbrellas of those other people hurrying along and who, as a consequence, ends up soaked.

I am the kind of woman who, when she is standing in the long queue for the 8.10 a.m. to Birmingham is always the one person other people make way for as they hurry their way across the open concourse of Euston station. They home in on me because they know I am the kind of woman who will step aside out of the queue to let them and their luggage and their friends and their children and their grandparents and their dog flock through, and when they have gone past and I move back to my vacated place, another flock of people immediately turns up so that I have to move aside yet again and am in a state of constant anxiety lest the queue should move forward without me.

I am the kind of woman who never makes a fuss, so if that were to happen I would meekly go to the very end of the queue and start all over again, but within seconds other travellers will identify me as that kind of woman and make for me as their hinged gate across the concourse.

I am the kind of woman who spends five minutes trying to decide which is the shortest queue for the cash till at the supermarket, or the booking window at the station or the clerk at the bank, only to find that the one I choose is the one with the slow learner cashier, or where the new roll of paper for the bill has to be changed and has got stuck in the machine, so someone in authority has to be called, or someone has pulled out from a concealed part of their person a dozen transparent bags of coins, each of which has to be counted and weighed.

I am the kind of woman who thinks a lot. I am the kind of woman who is tired of venturing forth into the jungle. I am the kind of woman who has decided not to go out any more. Not for the sort of reasons other people don't go out any more. Not simply because I'm afraid of being mugged or beaten or raped, although I am the kind of woman who is afraid of all those things. I am the kind of woman who could be knocked down by a car or a bus at any time; I am the kind of woman whose plane would crash, if I were the kind of woman who went anywhere by plane, and I am not that kind of woman.

I am the kind of woman who will not go out any more because of the eyes. The eyes tell me I am all wrong, that my hair blows in the wind when it should stay neat, that my nose gets red in the cold and my face red in the heat, that my skin freckles and peels in the summer, that I am scowling and I am the kind of woman who finds it far too much of a strain to smile smile smile.

I am the kind of woman who thinks a lot and resolves not to go out until I can clear a path and walk a straight line on the pavement without stepping off the kerb or aside to make way for anyone else, until I am the eyes which look and not the fearful thing looked at. I am the kind of woman who is going to stay in until all fear has gone.

I am the kind of woman who doesn't like staying in. I am the kind of woman who sits up late into the night listening to the central heating pipes cooling down, creaking and ticking, who hears the wood settle for the night, and is afraid to console it, for whom the sounds of the house going to sleep unsettle me out of my sleep. I am the kind of woman who doesn't like having the curtains open because then everyone can see in. I am the kind of woman who doesn't like having the curtains shut because then I can't see out.

I am the kind of woman who doesn't like having all the lights on because then everyone will know I am here and come and get me. I am the kind of woman who doesn't like having the lights off because then everyone will think the house is empty and break in. I am the kind of woman who mustn't spend too long in one room in case there is someone unwelcome in any of the other rooms. I am the kind of woman who mustn't spend too long in the lavatory because there you are really vulnerable.

I am the kind of woman who can't lie on her left side in bed because then her left ear won't hear anything, and who can't lie on her right side because then her right ear won't hear anything. I am the kind of woman who can't lie on her back because it is uncomfortable and I am the kind of woman who can't close her eyes because then she won't see someone walking into the room.

I am the kind of woman who stays up until dawn to hear the birds wake up and then when they are twittering can't get to sleep because of the noise.

I am the kind of woman who can never decide what to put on in the mornings, because trousers are too loose or too tight, skirts are too creased, everything is for best or doesn't fit.

I am the kind of woman who sometimes gets fed up with thinking morbid if true thoughts, and decides to go up the road to the shops to buy six eggs, which is quite enough for the kind of woman who eats an egg every day although she knows she shouldn't. I am the kind of woman who arrives in the shop to find there has been no delivery of eggs today.

I am the kind of woman who stands in the middle of the road in shock at the falling apart of her simple plan and then has to run quickly to the safety of the kerb because some silly person is driving too fast and dangerously and has hooted very loudly.

I am the kind of woman for whom there is nothing like a bit of anger and adrenalin, and I am the kind of woman who goes home and cleans the house furiously, lights, television and radio on and I am the kind of woman who says out loud, so that anyone who may be passing can overhear: 'Fuck 'em.' This time.

Cowrie

It starts with a sense of exile. The sea goes out a long way. The beach follows. The exile doesn't matter quite so much here on the beach, by the sea, where people don't matter quite so much. Where thoughts are heard against the feel of the waves, where the virgin, the cross, the words which cannot be spoken, where David and Goliath, those frightening men of strength, where even the puzzling Esther and the melancholy Ruth, are just sliding ridges under the cold sea.

Once two strands were joined. Once she found evidence that there was a connection between beaches, that they were so similar that no one could tell where one ended and another began, that the question of ending and beginning was not even a question. She is aware that this is romantic, that if it were ever really so, even if there is ample geological evidence to corroborate the idea, even then, the knowledge of it could only be there because now they were separate, distinct. But she is not a student of geology, she is not interested in the fact on the page, just in being here, in the cool wind and the hot sun and the bright focus down there on the sand.

The shell is lifted from its sandy counterpane, freed from the wet sand that nestles, sucks it close to the sand, that covers its ridged surface until only a small segment shows shady. The shell, lifted by the hand, shown to be imperfect, its edge jaggedly cut instead of regularly serrated, two perfect round holes in its rising mound, like animal bullet holes, the shell dropped from the hand in disappointment, the shell skittering and scudding along the sand, lifting and drifting edge-long in the warm autumn wind, a skittish shape, rejected because of its human idea of imperfection, itself careless and notionless, free and risky. A black fan shell on the beach at St Malo.

The same painstaking process reveals the sheer idea of partial perfection. Slightly smaller in size, with no bullet holes, complete, its miniature handle straight, a toy fan for a toy doll's house. The idea of perfection contained and defined by the empty hollow, where once there was another half, where the two halves contained a creature long dead or devoured. Such contradictions are embedded in the very idea of perfection, but like the shell itself embedded in the sand, implicit and only sometimes visible.

The black fan is carefully brought back to the English shore, kept in a room where the air and dryness turn the surface from shiny black to a dull, whitened dark grey. But the perfection of shape remains.

And this shell, hidden from sight, is a reminder of exile, of sea and of beach. Of the sea chill around her ankles, of wading in further and deeper until the water is warm around her knees and thighs and then further, a cold band of water holding her legs down, heavy, hard to pull along, and finally the solid tickle of water between her legs, shocking the base of her spine and then finally a cold layer takes her firmly round the middle of her body and she is in, the shoulders the last willing protesters and only her head above water. From now on she too is a shell, she floats and decides, she looks up at the blue sky and ahead at the rolling seas and she decides she will find her own shapes and images.

Out of the sea the sun is suddenly warmer, she squats on the sand, the sun warming her back, the backs of her thighs warming her calves. She searches beneath seaweed, and under small stones on the pale sand, she finds the cowrie, perfect, white and pale pink, her outer shell darkened slightly with fine dusts of sand, round to protect itself from the sea's sharp fling, no sharp edges like the black fan, no easy surface to be penetrated by bullet holes, too slippery for minute limpet-like creatures to parasite upon her. A tiny, tough, delicate creature, and after more searches and more searches a handful of the same, in a hand coated with sand which she holds cupped under the next wave which gathers the grains of sand back into itself, gently, respectfully until there is only a salty wet hand and the cowries at rest.

She stands and turns back to walk inshore. There are people on the beach, her heart jumps with the fear of the exile. Then she looks down at her loosely clasped hand and knows she is there, safe.

Meet My Mother

Once upon a time my mother was a mother just like any other mother. Once upon a time she couldn't bear not letting me know, on a regular basis, what she thought was wrong with the world, and in particular, wrong with me. What would make her happiest in the whole world, the happiest person in the whole wide world, is if I got married and settled down. Married and settled down. There's a sort of sticky inevitability about those words. Like marriage was a soufflé which had risen like a bird in the oven, and then as the cold air of settling down hit it, it would sink and sog its way back down into the dish from which it had first risen, all the air and light knocked out of it. Not, I may say, that I could use such a brilliant image in front of my mother, once upon a time. Oh no. If I had, her eyes would have glazed over, and she would have asked me if I wanted another cup of tea. Once upon a time I couldn't talk to my mother.

Once upon a time my mother's biggest crusade was to see me married and settled. Her crusade. I know it's probably a word from the wrong tradition, but it describes her fervour like no other word could. It was a sort of evangelism that was absolutely certain of itself. For her it wasn't a crusade, it was as normal and expected as breathing. Once upon a time.

Her favourite way, once upon a time, was to exert blackmail. Just for me, she would say. Just think of me. How can I die without having the pleasure of seeing you married, of having – Heaven Keep the Evil Eye from me – a grandchild. Or two. Or maybe, if I'm very lucky, three.

When my sister got married, I didn't hear the beginning or the end of it. White. How lovely she looked in white. How lovely I would look in white, white was always my favourite colour, she says to me. In fact, I never liked wearing white. In fact I hated wearing white. In fact, I never wore white, and she could not have failed to notice the fact. So when she tells me that white is my favourite colour, I think, thank you very much, you wait till I'm in the middle of my twenties, and I have all my fashion tastes and worries sorted out, and then you spring it on me that white is my favourite colour. Well, forget it. That's what I think, once upon a time, but of course I don't say it, because once upon a time I don't even bother to talk to my mother.

Then she'd use the cultural blackmail. My cousins got bar-mitzvahed and bat-mitzvahed – they're twins, a boy and a girl, and their parents are good liberal Jews – so she came back from the service and the party, and she said, oh, it was such a lovely service, and they even had a lady minister, and her mouth is curling a little in disapproval, but she's still trying to draw me back into the fold, a reverend lady, and she spoke so clear you could understand every word she said, and afterwards there was a reception in a most beautiful hotel, and the food – oh, there were horses doovers and fish and meat and coffee and I even shamed myself, she said, and took liberties with the wine, and then she giggled and then perhaps it was the wine taking liberties with her, but she leaned towards me and said – and I just listened to the innocence in her voice, and she said, Look, darling, if ever you want to arrange a function, and she's saying it so sweet, butter wouldn't melt in her mouth, if you ever want to arrange a function, you could do worse than choose that hotel. So I decide to match her innocence. And what sort of function would you have in mind, I ask? Oh, she says airily, waving her hand vaguely in the air, any function – a party, a wedding, anything.

A funeral, I say? That offends her. It's meant to. Don't joke, she says, her eyes suddenly serious. She turns away from me, and mock spits three times in the air, to warn away any bad devils who might take any of our words literally. A wedding, she says, you could do worse than have a wedding. At least then you would sleep legal.

There's no law about sleeping, I say, deliberately mis-understanding her, taking her literally. This is a game we have played since I was very young, in which each of us only listens to a little bit of what the other is saying, and this serves to keep the non-argument going until one of us gives in from sheer exhaustion at the other's pretended obtuseness.

You know what it says in the Book of Isaiah, she says. No, I don't, I counter. I've never read the Book of Isaiah, how should I know what it says? But I've committed a basic error in the invisible rules of our game, and she's won this one. Triumphant, she moves in for the kill: That's exactly the trouble with you, she says, you haven't read – I haven't read Proust, Mum, I say (I only call her Mum when I know I'm beaten). Feeble, I know. She is not impressed. I don't want to hear about your pagan habits, she yells, you should know what it is to be a Jew.

Once upon a time my mother used to talk like this. And each time, at a certain point, this is where we would end up. You should know what it is to be a Jew. Ever since I refused to go home for Pesach when I was eighteen – that was my first rebellion – and every time we have this row, we have to go through the *ganze megilla*, which, if she is fortified as now, with rather revolting sweet Israeli white wine, always ends with her in tears and me getting angry and saying nasty and cold and hurtful things, just to stop myself from collapsing into her arms and blubbering how sorry I am to be such a disappointment to her. So this time I resort to the safe family tactic and suggest we should have a cup of tea and put off the row to another time. That always works. As long as she feels I am still prepared to do battle in principle, she lets me off for the time being. She doesn't know that I have an ulterior motive. Something up my sleeve.

So when the tea is made and we are sipping it – me very kindly forebearing to point out that she is drinking tea with milk a mere hour after she has eaten meat – I decide to tell her.

'Mum,' I say. 'I've got something to tell you.'

'You're moving house again,' she suggests, conveying in her tone her wish that I should leave my semi-communal household.

'No. Something more important than that.'

'You could come and live at home again,' she says. 'I hoover your room every week. It's all ready for you. You just need clean sheets on the bed. I can do it for you in a minute.'

'Listen, Mother –' Now I'm getting serious and she knows it. By now my visit is full of little unfinished ends of conversation, like a half-unravelled sweater, with curly bits of wool sticking out in uncertain directions.

'I think I'm a lesbian,' I say.

'Pour me some more tea, dear,' she says. So I do. She adds milk, sugar, stirs it, slow as slow, while I watch her face and try to anticipate what will happen next. Silence.

'I've got a lover,' I try another tack.

'You should give up sugar,' she says, putting two spoons in her own cup. 'I read in *Woman's Own* it's bad for the heart.'

'It's a woman,' I say, determined now that she won't stop me.

'What is a woman?' she asks me, in a sort of mock-drunk, mock-philosophical tone, her eyelids heavy and portentous, as though she has just spoken after a silence of many years.

'My lover is a woman, Mummy.' Now I'm appealing to the time in her memory when I was the beautiful baby she likes to remember as perfect: clean, tidy, smiling, clever and precocious. 'My lover,' I say, just in case she hasn't quite got the point, 'is a lesbian.'

'Oh,' says my mother, enlightenment dawning in the upward inflection of her voice. 'What part of Lesbia is she from?'

I could kill her. I really could. Of all the mean, rotten, cheap jokes. And all the more rotten and mean and cheap because I give way and collapse into giggles.

'So whatever happened to the struggle with heterosexuality?' she adds, mocking, her eyes bright and alert.

'I have decided to give up heterosexuality. I have decided that, while the project of altering the balance of power within heterosexual relationships is still a valid one, it is no longer one I can espouse – so to speak. There is no revolutionary hope for the heterosexual, and I have therefore decided to love myself and become a lesbian.'

She sips her tea, looks up at me, and says, 'Just like that?'

'Almost,' I say, a little modest. What does she want, a blow by blow account?

She recovers her fire: 'You should have kept Brian on. He was a nice boy, and he was learning to cook nicely and he would have made a lovely father and helped you with the baby.'

I didn't know where to start. 'Brian? Father? Baby? What are you talking about? Brian was five years ago.'

'I liked him,' she says. 'He was almost like a son to me.'

'Yes, he used to bring his socks for you to darn,' I said, sarcastic.

'It's criminal the way people just throw things away nowadays. I believe in darning.' Her pronouncement for the day. I sighed. I knew this tack. She would go on to talk about the values of the olden days. 'In those days, we had a sense of values,' she says. 'The trouble with you young people is you have no sense of values.'

'That's what I've been trying to tell you,' I say. 'I value a relationship, and I'm trying to tell you about it.'

'You mean, you got a relationship?'

'Yes. I've been telling you.'

'I thought you just decided to be a lesbian.'

'It doesn't just happen like that,' I said.

'Oh. I thought you made a political decision,' she persists.

'Well, I did,' I say. 'But –'

And the rotten cow finishes my sentence for me. 'But you fancied someone,' she says, kind as anything.

'Yes,' I say, very lamely.

'Well,' she says, getting up from the table. I wonder what's coming next. 'Well, I shall just have to give you two scarves for Chanukah,' she says.

'She isn't Jewish, Mum,' I say. Well, that does it. She turns on me. 'You got to become a lesbian, you should at least have the decency to shack up with a nice Jewish girl. What would your father say if he was still alive?'

'Mum, how can I find a nice Jewish girl? *I'm* not a nice Jewish girl.'

'You're my daughter,' she says, still very angry, 'and you should know what upsets me. You should think about your mother.'

'I'm sorry, Mum.'

'You're sorry you're a lesbian, or you're sorry your girlfriend isn't Jewish?'

'I don't know. Yes. I do. I'm not sorry. That I'm a lesbian. I'm not at all sorry about that. I'm very pleased about that. And I'm not sorry Rowena's a – well, not Jewish.'

'Rowena.' She sniffs. 'What kind of a goyische name is that. Rowena.'

'Well, that's what I have to tell you, Mum.'

'And you're not sorry?'

'No.'

'Good. Then we know where we stand. You'll both come over for supper on Sunday night. I'll meet her.'

Well, I thought that was achievement enough. My

mother hadn't collapsed into a heap, hadn't killed herself, had invited me and Rowena round for supper.

Let me describe Rowena to you.

You remember in the first bit of the seventies it was all army reject dungarees and those American shoes, Kickers, they were called, and sort of tatty T-shirts and anything that didn't look positively dirty, but was somehow designed to give the effect of efficient, strong, functional being female-ness. Sort of army surplus-type gear. Then there was the punk era, and that rubbed itself off – if you'll pardon the phrase – on feminists, and all the floppy and dull-coloured gear was out, and Rowena, who has always spent at least half an hour every morning worrying about what the hell to wear – anti-government demo, or relative's wedding, it doesn't matter which – Rowena has dyed her hair a sort of cerise, with a deep purple streak down the middle, and she's wearing straight, tight black satin stretch trousers, with little black sequins stuck on at random, the sort of tight shiny trousers that make every curve and contour show, and she is so sexy. Really. I couldn't bear it the first day she went out looking like that. I wanted her all to myself. Anyway, then she has these silver high-heeled sandals, and this is the gear she's wearing to meet my mother. Oh, and she has a sort of luminous green and pink floppy T-shirt, sort of belted up round her bum. She and I have a bit of a to-and-fro, with me trying to persuade her to look a bit drab and oppressed, because that way we'll stand a better chance with my mother. The way Rowena looks in all that gear, she'll just confirm every terrible prejudice my mother has about *shicksas*, that they're all tarts and terrible seductions to nice Jewish boys – or in this case the nice Jewish girl she would like me to be. Piss off, says Rowena, kissing me lightly, so her lipstick doesn't smudge. I'm going to seduce your Mum, she says.

And honestly, she did. I don't mean literally, but just as we were going up the front steps, she twisted one of her ankles in those silly shoes, and somehow managed to rip a bit of the seam on the inside leg of her black trousers. So she arrives with a bit of white thigh showing, and almost before she's said a polite hello, she's asked my mother for a needle and thread. Mum couldn't have wanted a better introduction. She rushes for her sewing basket and before you know where you are, the two of them are deep in discussion about the relative merits of pure sanforised cotton or acrylic sewing yarn, and which works better for the machine and for what fabric – and within five minutes I was the odd one out, and I end up serving the food – chicken soup, and chicken with latkes (homemade, of course) and sweet and sour cabbage – oh, delicious stuff – I can taste it now – and of course they've finished with the sewing, they go on to the food. Rowena is into cooking Chinese food, and you'd think they would never run out of recipes to exchange. I end up turning the television on and falling asleep in front of Melvyn Bragg on the South Bank Show, doing a programme about lost African cultures.

Next thing, my mother is going off to an older women's group, and then she gets involved in pension rights, and she can't finish a skirt she's making for me because she has to go on a demonstration. Then she forgets my birthday. And why? Because she's going on a day trip to Greenham. She spends the entire day before making sandwiches, and God knows what to take with her, and she's so busy, she forgets my birthday. Well, of course, I didn't say anything. How could I, I've spent my whole life pooh-poohing rituals and occasions like that, and I always have to be reminded of everyone's birthday, so who am I to fall into a heap because my mother, who kept the family's birthdays religiously, and always sent a card – stupid cards with baskets of flowers on them, that kind of thing, but still, a card; how can I complain?

Then, one evening, when I have a local tenants' meeting to go to, I notice Rowena is getting all her war paint on, and when I ask her where she's going, she reminds me that it's the women's disco tonight, which I'd forgotten. So I chirp up, oh, I'll come on after the meeting, we can have a bop. And she's off-putting; I don't think I'll stay long enough, she says. Oh? You look as though you're dressed for a long siege, I say. And paranoia being my middle name, I ask her whether she's going with someone. Sort of, she says. Don't think I know her, I say, mock-contemplative. Sortov; no. She just arrived in this country, or something? In a manner of speaking, says Rowena. Actually – and she puts down her hair gel, the better to face me – I'm taking your mother. I promise you, I fell on to a chair with shock. My mother, at a women's disco, surrounded by – well, us. Rowena looks very apologetic; my mother, she says, was asking her about me, and my friends. And then my mother suggested having a quick look in at the women's disco. Rowena was quite adamant that the suggestion came from my mother.

The next thing, my mother goes punk. She dyed her hair green. Well, green highlights. Well, the first time I saw her, the way the light shone on her hair, it looked sort of bluey green. I suppose in the olden days it would have been what people called a blue rinse. All her friends think she's just had a blue rinse. But I know that really she's gone elderly punk.

Then, next thing, she's joined a Jewish feminist group, and after one meeting, she comes back all excited late at night and she phones me at midnight to harangue me for half an hour about how patriarchal the Judaeo-Christian heritage is, and have I really thought hard and long about the story of Eve in Genesis? Well, usually my reaction, when she asks me if I've read this or that book in the Old Testament, is to bridle and answer back, and this time is no different, and I come up with No, and I haven't read *War and Peace* either, and suddenly I hear myself, and I think, what am I saying, who am I talking to, so I pretend that my cocoa's boiling over and I hang up the phone and I sit there and have a little think.

Rowena's sitting up in bed reading a little light bedtime Foucault, and she can see I'm upset. She puts her book down and puts her arm round me, and I start talking.

'You must think I'm going round the twist. For years

I've been complaining about my mother, how she doesn't understand me, how bigoted she is, how I can't talk to her, how she makes me feel guilty, why can't I have a mother I can talk to like a friend, share things with, have the perfect socialist feminist mother-daughter relationship, instead of this fucked up bourgeois blackmail job. And now look at me. I'm upset when she forgets my birthday. I feel uncomfortable at the idea that she's going out and having a good time, I get stomach ache at the thought that she may go off cooking, I can't stand the way her house gets more and more untidy, because she's giving priority to other things. What on earth is the matter with me?'

Rowena pats me maternally on the shoulder. 'There are some,' she says, 'would say it was latent competition with your mother for your father that is making you unable to see your mother's actions as other than a direct threat.'

'Freudian garbage,' I say. Rowena shrugs, and indicates that she's a bit bored with the conversation and wants to get back to her book. I don't mind, really, because I don't want to talk anyway, I want to think.

So I think. I sit there and I think. And I think, once upon a time I had a mother who was just what she should be. Manipulative, bigoted, a pain in the neck, didn't understand me, didn't want to understand me, wanted me to be all the things she thought I should be. Once upon a time I could dread going round to visit her on Sunday, I could be on my guard against her attacks, and secretly I could enjoy eating her home-made biscuits, made with butter, delicious and crumbly, and I could take material round for her to make clothes for me, and borrow a knitting pattern from her, and this was our exchange. Once upon a time I had a mother. Now she's gone. And I don't know what I'm going to do.

Perhaps I'll talk to Rowena again. In the morning.

Two: Mothers, Music and the Transformation of Texts

For in the beginning of literature is the myth, and in the end as well.

'Parable of Cervantes and the *Quixote*'
by Jorge Luis Borges,
translated by James E. Irby.
(*Labyrinths*, Penguin, 1981)

Singer's Geese

This is a jewel of a story. Such a jewel of a story that I want to wear it in my own way so that you can see it and share in its beauty, because I have been wearing it inside my mind for a long time, ever since I first read it.

The story happened to someone else. More precisely, it happened to someone else's mother. To the mother of Isaac Bashevis Singer, the writer, the American writer, the American Jewish writer, the American Jewish writer who came from Poland and who writes in Yiddish which is translated into English. I could tell you a lot more about him, but that would take up a lot of space and I want to get to the story which is part of a whole lot of stories which he tells about growing up as a boy in Warsaw. In the book where he tells all these stories, he shows us what sort of questions he asked as a boy. Questions like, What would happen if a bird flew in the same direction forever? And, If a star is so big, bigger than the earth, how is it, he asks, that it fits in the narrow strip of sky that I can see from my bedroom window?

I like those questions, because even when you know the

correct and scientific answer, you can still ask the question again and still want to know a different answer.

I'll tell this story in my own way, after Isaac Bashevis Singer; 'after' in the sense of 'after I have read it', and 'after' in the sense of 'in the footsteps of'. And if my footprints are a slightly different shape, then that is the way it always is with stories.

Isaac Bashevis Singer calls the story 'Why the geese shrieked'. Oh, before I tell you about the geese, you know about chickens? You know the way chickens will run and squawk at anything. Chickens are really very silly creatures, although we once had a chicken which would let me stroke her on the back. I never understood why, because she didn't behave like a pet in any other way. Anyway, with chickens, when you catch them, the way you do it is, you grab at their legs and then when you've got them by both legs, you hold them upside down and their wings splay out to the side like two beautiful feather fans and in this position they are quite quiet because they have enough of a sense of self preservation not to struggle in case they damage their wings and feet. If you want them to lie still on the ground you have to tie their feet together.

Now geese are not at all like that. You don't have to tie their feet at all. They will stand on their patch of straw in the market waiting to be sold. When the dog barks at them, to make sure they don't wander off, they get angry and stick their necks straight out and hiss. Anyway, they are usually too fat to waddle very far, especially those who have been force-fed for pâté de foie gras.

Anyway, the story goes that Isaac Bashevis Singer's parents were at home when a neighbour comes round, carrying a heavy basket and in a great state, in such a state that her *sheitl* (the wig that orthodox married Jewish women have to wear) is all to one side and she hasn't even noticed. She puts the basket down and then she realises about the wig, so she straightens it and then she says, 'Mr Singer, I got a problem.'

'Oh,' says Mr Singer, 'how can I help you?'

'Well,' she says. 'It's these two geese.' And she shows him she's got two dead geese in the basket.

So Mrs Singer says, 'So what is wrong with the geese?'

So the neighbour says, 'Look, the geese were properly killed, it was all kosher, I watched it being done, the *shochet* killed them, then he held them down so all the blood would run away, then he put them on the ground, and when they stopped flapping around, I took them into the kitchen and I cut off their heads, I took out the *kishkas*, the guts, the livers, everything – and now I'm scared.'

'What are you scared of?' asks Mrs Singer.

'I'm scared of the geese,' says the neighbour. 'They're dead and they keep shrieking.'

Well, Mrs Singer has a little laugh. 'Dead geese don't shriek,' she says.

'You don't believe me?' says the neighbour. 'All right, then, you listen for yourself.'

And she takes the two dead geese out of the basket and puts them on the table. 'There you are,' she says. 'Two ordinary dead geese.'

'That's right,' says Mrs Singer. 'You're not going to tell me they shriek.'

So the neighbour takes one goose and she hurls it against the other, and there is a shriek, like the cackling of a goose only much higher. Mr Singer is very taken aback at this, he thinks perhaps this is a sign from the Evil One.

'Well,' says the neighbour. 'Now what do you say?'

And she hurls one goose against the other and again they can hear the sound. And Mr Singer starts praying, and the neighbour starts crying and complaining, and then Mrs Singer cuts across all this and she says to the neighbour, 'Tell me, did you remove their windpipes?'

And the neighbour says, 'Their windpipes? No, I didn't.'

And so Mrs Singer takes one of the geese, pushes her fingers inside its body and with all her strength pulls the thin tube that leads from the neck to the lungs. And then she does the same thing with the other goose, and then she says 'There. Now see if they shriek.'

And as Mrs Singer stands there with her hands all bloody, the neighbour takes one goose and hurls it against the other. Nothing happens.

'There,' says Mrs Singer, and gets a wet cloth to wipe her hands clean.

'Well, it is a mystery to me,' says Mr Singer.

'I don't understand it,' says the neighbour.

'There is no mystery,' says Mrs Singer. 'There is always an explanation for everything. Dead geese don't shriek.'

'Can I take them home and cook them now?' asks the neighbour.

'Of course,' says Mrs Singer. 'They won't make a sound in your pot.'

And so the neighbour takes her geese home and Mr and Mrs Singer get on with whatever they are doing and neither of them says anything, but perhaps each of them envies the other one just a little bit.

Return to Sender

(Adapted from a section of *Daniel Deronda* by George Eliot)

Come in.

I do apologise for arriving here two days later than I said I would, in my letter to you. But no doubt you have had ample time to see round Genoa, perhaps even take a boat, so that you might enjoy the magnificent view of the city and the harbour from the sea.

Do sit down.

Whenever I see the grand harbour, I imagine the multi-tudinous Spanish Jews, centuries ago, driven destitute from their Spanish homes, suffered to land from the crowded ships only for a brief rest on this grand quay of Genoa, overspreading it with a pall of famine and plague – dying mothers with dying children at their breasts; fathers and sons agaze at each other's haggardness, like starving prisoners turned out beneath the midday sun.

I imagine that the colourless wording of my letter gave you no clue as to what might be in store for you. I imagine also, that Sir Hugo has been correctly reticent and not anticipated any of my disclosures. Yes. I thought so.

It is hot here at noon. The oleanders in the tubs along the wayside gardens look more and more like fatigued holiday-makers, and the roads get deeper with dry, white dust. I love the evenings, the scattering abroad of all those whom the midday sun has sent under shelter, the tinkling of mule bells, light footsteps and voices; the buildings, forts and castles, seem to come forth and gaze in fullness of beauty after their long siesta, till all strong colour melts in the stream of moonlight, which makes the streets a new spectacle, with shadows, both still and moving; and then the moon descends slowly into deep night and silence, and nothing shines but the port lights of the great Lanterna in the blackness below, and the glimmering stars in the blackness above.

I have told the servants that you are a doctor whom I am consulting. They are not surprised to know that you have met me here, in the library, in the cool of the evening. They may be a little surprised, however, to see someone so young, so vibrant. An eminent physician, whom I have come to Genoa to consult. So vibrant.

'To my son, Daniel Deronda: I shall be in Genoa on the fourteenth of this month. My health is shaken and I desire there should be no time lost before I deliver to you what I have long withheld. Bring with you the diamond ring Sir Hugo gave you. I shall like to see it again. Your unknown mother, Leonora Halm-Eberstein.'

You may rest assured that the love Sir Hugo bears you will not be altered by anything.

You are a beautiful creature. I knew you would be. You are blushing. Yet you are not overcome with emotion. You must have lived through so many ideal meetings with me. No doubt they all seemed more real than this. Perhaps you can see some likeness to your own face in mine? You have a painful sense of aloofness about you.

I suppose you must have begun to wonder about the mysteries of your parentage. Well. I am your mother. But you can have no love for me. I have not the foolish notion that you can love me merely because I am your mother. I thought I chose something better for you than being with me. I did not think I deprived you of anything worth having. I don't mean to speak ill of myself, but I had not much affection to give you. I did not want affection. I had been stifled with it. I wanted to live out the life that was in me, and not to be hampered with other lives. I was a great singer, and I acted as well as I sang. All the rest were poor beside me. Men followed me from one country to another. I was living a myriad lives in one. I did not want a child.

I have cast all precedent out of my mind in telling you this. Precedence has no excuse for me. I can only seek a justification in the words I can find for my experience. I did not want to marry. I was forced to marry your father – forced, I mean, by my father's wishes and commands. And besides, it was my best way of getting some freedom. I could rule my husband but not my father. I had a right to be free. I had a right to seek my freedom from a bondage that I hated. And the bondage that I hated for myself, I wanted to keep you from. What better could the most loving mother have done? I relieved you from the bondage of having been born a Jew. I chose for you what I would have chosen for myself. You are an English gentleman. I secured you that.

Why did I do it? When you are as old as I am, then it will not seem so simple a question. People talk of their motives in a cut and dried way. Every woman is supposed to have the same set of motives, or else to be a monster. I am not a monster, but I have not felt exactly what other women feel – or say they feel, for fear of being thought unlike others. When you reproach me in your heart for sending you away from me, you mean I ought to say I felt about you as other women feel about their children. I did not feel that. I was glad to be freed from you.

Do I seem now to be revoking everything? Well, there are reasons. I feel many things I can't understand. A fatal illness has been growing in me for a year. I will not deny anything I have done. I will not pretend to love where I have no love. But shadows are rising round me. If I have wronged the dead – I have but little time to do what I have left undone.

Your grandfather never comprehended me, or if he did, he only thought of fettering me into obedience. I was to be what he called 'the Jewish woman' under pain of his curse. I was to feel everything I did not feel, and believe everything I did not believe. I was to feel awe for the bit of parchment in the *mezzuza* over the door; to dread lest a bit of butter should touch a bit of meat, to think it beautiful that men should bind *tephillin* on them and women not – to adore the wisdom of such laws, however silly they might seem to me. I was to love the long prayers in the ugly synagogue, and the howling and the gabbling and the dreadful fasts and the tiresome feasts, and my father's endless discoursing about Our People, which was a thunder without meaning in my ears. But I did not care at all. I cared for the wide world, and all that I could represent in it. I hated living under the shadow of my father's strictness. Teaching, teaching, 'this you must be', 'that you must not be', pressed on me like a frame that got tighter and tighter as I grew. I wanted to live a large life, with freedom to do what everyone else did, and be carried along in a great current. You are glad to have been born a Jew? That is because you have not been brought up as a Jew. That separateness seems sweet to you because I saved you from it.

I am still the same Leonore; within me is the same desire, the same will, the same choice. But there are new events – feelings, apparitions in the darkness. We only consent to what we love. I am obeying something tyrannic. I am forced to be withered, to feel pain, to be dying slowly. Do I love that?

I have been forced to obey my dead father. I have been forced to tell you that you are a Jew.

You can never imagine what it is to have a man's force of genius in you, and yet to suffer the slavery of being a girl. To have a pattern cut out – this is the Jewish woman, this is what you must be. A woman's heart must be of such a size, else it must be pressed small, like Chinese feet. Her happiness is to be made, as cakes are, by a fixed receipt. My father wished me to have been a son; he cared for me as a makeshift link. He hated the idea that Jewish women should be thought of by the Christian world as some sort of material to make public singers and actresses of. As if we were not the more enviable for that. That is a chance of escaping from bondage.

I don't deny that your grandfather was a good man, and a clever physician. A man to be admired in a play – grand, with an iron will. But such men turn their wives and daughters into slaves. They would rule the world if they could, but not ruling the world, they throw the weight of their will on the necks and souls of women. But nature sometimes thwarts them. My father had no other child than his daughter, and she was like himself.

Your father was different. Unlike me – he was all loving-ness and affection. I knew I could rule him; and I made him secretly promise me, before I married him, that he would put no hindrance in the way of my being an artist. My father was on his deathbed when we were married; from the first he had fixed his mind on my marrying my cousin Ephraim. And when a woman's will is as strong as the man's who wants to govern her, half her strength must be concealment. I meant to have my will in the end, but I could only have it by seeming to obey. I had an awe of my father. I hated to feel awed. I wished I could defy him openly, but I never could. It was what I could not imagine: I could not act it to myself that I should begin to defy my father openly and succeed. And I never would risk failure.

My mother was English – a Jewess of Portuguese descent. My father married her in England; through that marriage my father thwarted his own plans. My mother died when I was eight years old, and then my father allowed me to be continually with my aunt Leonora, here in Genoa, and be taught under her eyes. My father did not hinder it; but I saw it again and again in my father, that he did not guard against consequences because he felt sure he could hinder them if he liked. That I was taught music and singing meant nothing to him. He meant that I should obey his will and marry my cousin. My father died three weeks after we were married and then I had my way. It has not lasted, though. My father is getting his way now.

I think perhaps there is something of your own father in you. He was devoted to me. As I loved the life of my art, so he loved me. Let me look at the ring on your hand. It was your father's ring.

Look how like mine your hand is.

Do not look so distressed. I am suffering, but with a suffering that you cannot comfort. I did not send for you to comfort me. I do not expect anything from you.

Sir Hugo tells me that you have a wonderful mind; you are wiser than he is, with all his sixty years. I think you are glad to know that you were born a Jew. Well. Your feelings are against mine. You cannot thank me for what I did. You owe me no duties. It is better so.

When your father died, I resolved that I would have no more ties. Sir Hugo Mallinger was one who courted me, who wished to marry me. He was madly in love with me. One day I asked him, 'Is there a man capable of doing something for love and expecting nothing in return?' He said, 'What is it you want done?' I said, 'Take my boy and bring him up as an Englishman, and let him never know anything about his parents.' You were little more than two years old. I had not meditated much on the plan beforehand, but as soon as I spoke of it, it took possession of me as something I could not rest without doing. At first he thought I was not serious, but I convinced him. He agreed that it would be for your good. A great singer and actress is a queen, but she gives no royalty to her son. Afterwards, I made Sir Hugo a trustee of your fortune. And I had a joy in doing it. You were my son and it was for me to say what you should be. I said you should not know you were a Jew.

It was no shame to me. I have rid myself of the Jewish tatters and gibberish that make people nudge each other at the sight of us as if we were tattooed under our clothes, though our faces are as whole as theirs. I delivered you from the pelting contempt that pursues Jewish separateness. I am not ashamed of what I did.

Before I married the second time I was baptised. I made myself like the people I lived among. I had a right to do it. I was not like a brute, obliged to go with my own herd.

I have not repented. But yet – it is illness. I don't doubt that it has been illness. My mind has gone back. It has all come fast. Sometimes I am in an agony of pain – I daresay I shall be tonight. Then it is as if all the life I have chosen to live, all thoughts, all will, forsook me and left me alone with my memories, and I can't get away; the pain seems to keep me there. My childhood – my girlhood – the day of my marriage – the day of my father's death – there seems to be nothing since. Then a great horror comes over me. What do I know of life or death? And what my father called 'right' may be a power that is laying hold of me – that is clutching me now. Well, I will satisfy him. I cannot go into the darkness without satisfying him. I have hidden what was his.

Often, when I am at ease, it sinks away, my whole self comes back. But I know that the other will come back – the poor, solitary, forsaken remains of self that can resist nothing. And now you have made it worse for me – but I shall have told you everything. And what reproach is there against me, since I have made you glad to be a Jew? I hoped you would have become a proud Englishman, who resented being touched by a Jew. I wish you had been.

I meant never to marry again. I meant to be free and to live for my art. I had parted with you. I had no bonds. For nine years I was a queen. I enjoyed the life I had longed for. But something strange befell me. I began to sing out of tune. It was like a fit of forgetfulness. People told me of it. It was horrible to me. I could not bear the prospect of failure and decline. Another woman was thrusting herself in my place. The world of art and beauty is also a place of cruelty and ruthlessness. I was driven to marry. I made believe that I preferred being the wife of a Russian noble to being the greatest lyric actress of Europe. I made believe – I acted the part. It was because I felt my greatness sinking away from me. I would not wait till people said, 'She had better go'. My husband and other children do not know of your existence.

I can bear no more now. You see, I had no life left to love you with. That singing out of tune passed – it was like an illness – but it was too late. I could not go back. I need nothing that the skill of man can give me. But perhaps now that I have satisfied my father's will, your face will come to me in my dreams, instead of his – your young, loving face.

I have told you everything that could be demanded of me, I think. And now, we must part. You could not love me. Don't deny it. You don't like what I did. You are angry with me. You think I have robbed you of something. You are, perhaps, on your grandfather's side and may condemn me in your heart. But you would be wrong to be angry with me. You are the better for what I did. And yet – and yet . . .

My father never thought of me except as an instrument. Because I had wants outside his purpose, I was to be put in a frame and tortured. If that is the right law for the world, I will not say I love it. If my acts were wrong – if it is God who is exacting from me that I should deliver up what I withheld – who is punishing me because I deceived my father – well, I have told everything. I have done what I could. And your soul consents. That is enough. I have, after all, been the instrument of my father's desires. 'I desire a grandson who shall have a true Jewish heart.'

I wanted to thwart my father. And you would have me love what I have hated from the time I was so high. That can never be. We must part and not see one another again. You are angry that I banished you. You reproached me that I parted with you when you were small, and now you are come back to me and I cannot make you a joy. Have you the cursing spirit of the Jew in you? Are you not able to forgive me? Shall you be glad to think that I am punished because I was not a Jewish mother to you?

You shall give up nothing. You will be happy. You shall let me think of you as happy. I shall have done you no harm. You have no reason to curse me. You shall feel for me as they feel for the dead whom they say prayers for – you shall long that I may be freed from all suffering – from all punishment. If you think Kaddish will help me, then say it. And I shall see you instead of always seeing your grandfather. You will come between me and the dead. When I am in your mind, you will look as you do now – always, as if you were a tender son – always – as if I had been a tender mother.

Take this portrait – this miniature of me, as I was in my youth, full of fire and promise. There. When I was young, I looked for the blending of a complete personal love in one current with a larger duty. Perhaps you will do the same.

Goodbye, my son. We shall hear no more of each other. Kiss me.

At daybreak Anshel's mother-in-law and her band descended upon the marriage chamber and tore the bedsheets from beneath Hadass to make sure the marriage had been consummated. When traces of blood were discovered, the company grew merry and began kissing and congratulating the bride. Then, brandishing the sheet, they flocked outside and danced a kosher dance in the newly fallen snow. Anshel had found a way to deflower the bride.

'Yentl the Yeshiva Boy'
by Isaac Bashevis Singer.
(*The Penguin Collected Stories of Isaac Bashevis Singer*, Penguin, 1981)

Anshel's Story

I had a wonderful and sad dream. I dreamed that I was dressed as a man and that everyone thought I was a man, although I knew I was a woman. I am not sure why I dressed as a man, but it may have had something to do with the books I was carrying. Anyway, I was studying with other young men, and I made friends with Avigdor, an intense, dark young man. Every time I saw him my heart would jump. We studied together, we debated, we argued, we ate together. Then one day he confided in me that he was in love with a young woman called Hadass, but that he was forbidden to marry her. She too loved him, he said. When he told me about it, outwardly I was a sympathetic friend, but inwardly I was hot and cold and furious and devils crawled around my brain telling me to rip his clothes and to scratch his face and pull his beard.

This frightened me, and I was determined to catch a glimpse of this Hadass, of whom just the mention produced such desires for violence. So I got into the habit of taking walks past her house in order to see her, and one day I was rewarded. There she was, a tall, intense, dark-haired young woman. The moment I saw her in the street I knew it was she, and as we walked past one another my heart jumped in exactly the same way as it did when I saw Avigdor.

As we passed, I looked at her and she looked at me. She blushed with great surprise that a young man such as myself should look her straight in the eyes, because it is forbidden; I was also surprised that she should look me straight in the eyes, but I knew I did not blush, because I had so many secrets within me that something as small as this could not discomfort me.

The dream ended here. The next night I had another dream. This time Avigdor was unhappily married to someone else, and I was betrothed to Hadass. I married Hadass, and no one caught on that I was a woman, not even Hadass. Don't ask me how this is possible; remember, this was a dream and in dreams all things are possible. In the dream I heard someone saying, 'Anshel had found a way to deflower the bride' – but more than that I cannot tell you.

Avigdor and I continued to study together and my heart continued to jump when I saw him. He grew more and more unhappy, since he was still in love with Hadass. Eventually I could bear his unhappiness no longer. I told him that I was a woman, that the marriage between myself and Hadass could not be valid, and that if I divorced her, and Avigdor divorced his wife, perhaps this time the two of them could find happiness together. Avigdor was very taken aback by it all, but eventually he agreed, and this is what happened.

On the third night I dreamed that I was walking on a long road, out of the town, leaving behind me the sound of the marriage celebrations between Hadass and Avigdor, and hearing voices gossip about me: 'He fell into the hands of Catholic priests and was converted', 'He has fallen for another woman', 'He has been carried away by evil spirits', 'Perhaps he was an evil spirit himself. He never went to the bathhouse or the river with the other young men. It is well known that demons have the feet of geese. Has anyone ever seen him barefoot? Well, then.'

On the fourth night I dreamed that Avigdor and Hadass were celebrating the birth of their first child, a boy. At the circumcision Avigdor named him 'Anshel', after me, to the shock of all the assembled people.

Now these dreams upset me. It seemed to me that although it looked like a happy ending, there were all sorts of questions I wanted to ask in the dreams. For example, when Avigdor learned that Anshel was a woman, why didn't he throw convention to the winds and marry her? After all, Avigdor liked and loved Anshel and had more in common with him/her than with anyone else, and this was something much stronger than the remote desire and lust which he felt for Hadass. He didn't know Hadass, he had never been in a room alone with her, he had never had a conversation with her, he could not possibly know how her mind, her spirit, matched with her beautiful exterior.

Then there was Anshel. Why was Anshel so self-sacrificing? When Anshel revealed himself to be a woman, why did she not, in keeping with her determination to study and live the life she wanted – why did she not pursue it and show Avigdor that they were made for one another? Why couldn't they have left the town and gone away somewhere together?

Then again, why did Anshel's heart jump when she saw Hadass for the first time? How did Anshel find a way to deflower Hadass?

And Hadass. What did Hadass really think of Anshel? What did Hadass feel about Anshel? Was Hadass really so ignorant that she did not know that Anshel was not a man? What happened when Anshel had her period?

These are silly questions, because dreams do not answer questions. They just ask them, and then your life must live out the answers.

But I could not rest, I could not sleep, I lost interest in my food, I grew careless about my appearance, I found excuses to stay at home, prowling around the house, wondering, worrying, asking, asking, trying to understand why I should have dreamed these things, and why they should worry me so.

My friends began to be concerned, to telephone, to write letters, to come round. In the end I tore out the telephone, bolted the door and left all the letters unopened on the mat. After two weeks in this way, I fell into a long sleep, and I began to dream again, a number of dreams. One after the other.

In the first dream, someone was sitting by my bed. I don't know who it was. A voice said, 'Yentl knew she wasn't cut out for a woman's life.' I got up and put on the clothes lying by my bed. Black trousers, a fringed prayer shawl, a silk coat, a skullcap, a velvet hat. I looked at myself in the mirror. A dark, intense young man. My hair was short, with sidecurls beside my ears. I liked what I saw. I was a young man who had not yet started shaving. There was a slight down on my upper lip, considered unsightly if I were a woman, but in keeping with the young brightness in my male eyes.

I left my house and went to the place where the young men studied. Here I met my friend Avigdor. We argued about a particularly thorny section of the Talmud, and then, because we were hot and tired and annoyed with one another, because we could not agree, one of us, I cannot tell you which, suggested we should go down to the river to swim.

The sun was hot, and as we walked away from the houses and the people, our annoyance with each other abated. We stopped in the shade of a clump of trees. We did not speak. We began to undress, a few feet away from one another. Then a warm gust of wind caught my hat and blew it across to Avigdor and he caught it, and I ran after it, across the soft grass, and as I took the hat from him our hands touched and we looked at one another, full in the face, and then we both smiled and then we both laughed and dropped the hat and clasped each other's hands, and I kissed his hand and put it against my cheek, and then he did the same. And then we finished undressing and we dived into the river, and there, under the water, where we could not be seen by any prying eyes, and where we ourselves did not need to

71

look, we found each other's bodies, and swam and felt and touched and all the arguing fell away and there was nothing but sun and sparkling water, and I knew that for us both this was a way of being men for which there was no shame and no need to wonder or worry.

When we came out of the water, again we did not speak. As we walked back towards the town, Avigdor said to me, 'I shall never marry', and I said, 'Nor shall I', and then we returned to our life of study. We knew we could always return to the river.

In the second dream I was studying beside Avigdor. He was smoking a cigarette, and took it from his mouth to give me a puff. I gave him a buckwheat cake which I had bought that morning. Then Avigdor buttoned up his coat because it was cold and one of his buttons fell off. So I took a needle and thread from my pocket and sewed it on again. Avigdor looked very closely at me and said, 'But I thought you told me you couldn't sew?' I didn't say anything. Later we went to lie on the grass and Avigdor said, 'Why can't a woman be like a man?'

And I said 'Questions, questions, always questions,' and then I got up and ran off down to the river, with Avigdor following me, and when we got there he was out of breath and I went to a clump of bushes, and I began to undress, and he said, 'You're not going swimming, are you? It's nearly dark, the water will be freezing', and I said nothing and I undressed and then I said, 'I am not a man, I am a woman and I love you', and he came to me and went to put his arms round me and I held him back from me and said he must undress too and he did, and it was the first time either of us had seen the body of someone from the opposite sex and we made love there, with no more speaking, in the way that a man and a woman who have known each other very well for a long time do. And then we dressed and went back to the town. And of course, being a dream, we knew there was no fear of my getting pregnant.

In the third dream I was betrothed to Hadass. Somehow I knew that I was going through with the marriage for

Avigdor's sake, as if I somehow believed that once Hadass and I were married, my love for my friend would be so great that he would simply appear in the marriage bed in my stead, that he would become me and find true happiness. I was being measured for my wedding suit, and I had to find all sorts of excuses to measure myself, lest the tailors discover that I was a woman and not a man. The account of the wedding was engraved in gold in my dream, as if I were reading it from a silver screen:

'On the day of the wedding . . . the bridegroom delivered a Talmudic discourse, and the rest of the company argued the points while smoking cigarettes and drinking wine, liqueurs, tea with lemon or raspberry jam. Then followed the ceremony of veiling the bride, after which the bridegroom was led to the wedding canopy that had been set up at the side of the synagogue. The night was frosty and clear, the sky full of stars. The musicians struck up a tune. Two rows of girls held lighted tapers and braided wax candles. After the wedding ceremony the bride and groom broke their fast with golden chicken broth. Then the dancing began . . . After the virtue dance the bride and groom were led separately to the marriage chamber. The wedding attendants instructed the couple in the proper conduct and enjoined them to "be fruitful and multiply".'

Hadass stood shyly by the bed when I came into the room. I went up to her and took her hand. She let me. I said, Hadass, this isn't going to be easy for either of us. I know what has to be done, she said, I hope you will not be disappointed in me.

I smiled. I had decided that this was the moment of judgement. After such a long time, during which I had been dogged by feelings of guilt, I knew that I could not go any further unless I told Hadass the truth. But I did not know why. I just knew that every word she spoke was true, but with an irony she could not possibly understand. But then, I thought to myself, this is the life for which Hadass has been prepared. She has been brought up not to understand the world of books, the world of study, the world of managing the world; she has been brought up to understand only the running of a house, and those actions of prayer which are allowed to women. Every morning her father thanks God that he was not born a woman. It was against that that I put on men's clothes, passed as a man, rejected all womanly actions which could have any kind of domestic possibility, it was because I refused to be the kind of woman men feared and rejected as a possibility for themselves. And now, here I stood, holding Hadass's hand, wondering how I would tell her.

'We should go to bed,' she said.

'Yes,' I answered.

We both paused. She smiled again. 'Will you undress first?' I asked.

'I think we should both undress together,' she said. 'Or I have an even better idea. We can undress one another.'

'I'm not sure –' I began.

'Oh,' she said, 'are you shy, then, Anshel?' If I had not known her to be the shy demure bride she was, I could have sworn she was teasing me. One thing was for sure, I didn't want her undressing me. I wanted to be in charge of everything I revealed.

She began undoing her dress. I watched. My heart jumped as she took it off, sliding it down to the floor. I looked at her.

'The first time we met you looked straight at me,' she said.

'I'm sorry,' I answered, and turned my back. I was really frightened now. I heard more clothes being removed behind me. I couldn't look round. My hands were sweating. Then there was a silence, and I jumped. She was standing behind me, her arms round me. I knew she was naked. She began to undo my jacket. I was paralysed. I let her. She slipped the jacket off my shoulders and let it fall onto the floor. I was shivering.

'You're cold,' she said, and I could feel her breath on my neck. Then she moved closer and I could feel her body pressed against my back. Once more her arms came round me, undid my shirt, and she slid her hands under all my garments and moved them gently, curiously over my breasts.

'I thought so,' she said, her breath against my neck.

'Thought so what?' My voice was thin, strange.

'I thought you were someone else,' she said, her hands feeling, exploring, changing.

'I don't understand,' I said. 'I am Anshel.'

'Oh yes,' she said. 'Of course you are. And I am Hadass. Unless you would like to call me by another name.'

'What are you going to do?' I asked.

'I don't know,' she said. 'No one told me what to do in a situation like this. I suppose I can just go on feeling you – that is, if you don't mind –'

'Don't mind – Hadass –' I was finding it very difficult to stay standing up, to face away from her, I wanted to turn round, fling the rest of my clothes off, without losing touch of her, go to bed – and – I don't know what – but I felt we had to talk, to come to some rational decision – 'Hadass, listen for a moment.' Her hands stayed still.

'We cannot be married. We are two women.'

'Good,' she said. And her hands started moving again. I clasped my hands over hers, succeeding only in feeling more strongly, more clearly the warm pressure of her fingers.

'Just a second, Hadass. What are we going to say?'

'Say?'

'Tomorrow. What are we going to say to everyone?'

'It's not tomorrow I'm worried about, Anshel. It's tonight. Every girl worries about her wedding night. But then, of course, you wouldn't know that, being a young man and everything.'

'I'm sure young men worry as well.'

'Sure, are you? I wonder how you can be sure of that. I wonder, actually, how you can be sure of anything.'

'I know I'm in your power, Hadass. I just want to explain everything and then go away, leave you in peace.'

'You don't want to go away. You're tired. You want to go to bed. Come on, Anshel.'

I broke away from her and turned round. She stood, naked, beautiful. I felt ugly, heavy in my clothes. I took my shirt off. She watched me.

'There, you see,' she said, as I undressed. 'You're tired, it's been a long day, we can't possibly go out and say anything to anyone tonight, so we may as well get into bed and leave any real decision until tomorrow morning.'

She turned round and went to the bed, blew out the candle and I heard the rustling of the sheets, then a couple of pats, as if she was inviting me to join her. I got into bed, and immediately, without either of us speaking a word we put our arms round one another, and kissed and kissed, neither of us practised, each of us learning as we went and learning quickly, and without another word for a long time we forgot yesterday and we forgot others and we forgot tomorrow.

And afterwards, we lay there and talked. She told me that she had guessed I was a woman. How? Oh, she couldn't really tell. The way I smelled, she thought. Women's sweat smells different from men's sweat. Sometimes, anyway. She thought she could see the curve of my breasts through my clothes. But through so many layers? And I could have been plump. No, she shook her head, I wasn't plump. She had a feeling. And sometimes, something about the sway of my walk, a lightness that was not fitting for a serious young religious student. Why, then, hadn't she said anything? She shrugged. What was the point? She knew she would never have any choice, she had wanted to marry Avigdor and she had been prevented. What else would she ever do, other than obey what was laid down for her.

And – I was trying to find a way to ask a very difficult question, but her hand came snaking up over my body and I left it – or rather I changed it to a statement: 'We desired each other without knowing it,' I said. 'Oh, I knew it,' she answered. 'You didn't, because you were a woman masquerading as man, and to retain something of your identity you felt you could only desire a man in your heart, in secret.' 'You know I was in love with Avigdor too?' I asked, beginning to wonder if she was a witch, perhaps if there really were such things as witches. She shook her head. No, she didn't know who exactly, but she wasn't surprised it was Avigdor.

And then we both looked at one another and burst out laughing. We had loved one another and here we were, both talking about being in love with Avigdor. We both saw the joke at exactly the same moment. It was the last piece of unfinished business and we both realised we were exhausted. Just before we fell asleep one of us – I can't remember who – said, 'What about the sheet in the morning' and before we had time to think about it, we were both fast asleep.

The next morning we were woken by clamouring outside the room. It was Hadass's mother and her friends waiting to come into the room and take the sheet from the bed to make sure the marriage had been consummated. I jumped up in terror, sure now that terrible things would happen, that we would be punished for what we had done the previous night – but as Hadass and I both got out of bed quickly and grabbed for our clothes, we noticed blood on the sheet. We looked at each other and we grinned. Last night was not a mistake and now one of us, we did not yet know which one, and it might even have been both of us, had somehow ordered our bodies to menstruate.

We dressed, Hadass in a demure dress, me in my suit, and everything was duly and formally celebrated.

After this dream I woke up. I felt refreshed, happy, drew the curtains, bathed, washed my hair, ate breakfast, tidied the house and began to go about my life again as before. But after a while I began to feel anxious again. I was sleeping deep, dreamless nights, waking up fresh and vital, but I felt that there was something unfinished. I began to think about it during the day. I knew there was another dream somewhere which I had to have before the experience could be put behind me. And it was one of three possibilities.

In the first possibility Hadass and I lived happily ever after in subterfuge. That we never had children was a source of much real anguish to her family and much pretended anguish on our part. Our secret kept us warm. When we were alone we shared all domestic tasks, and I taught her from my studies until she could argue as well as anyone.

In the second possibility we felt we could not keep up the charade, and I left, invented a divorce and Hadass married Avigdor, whom she still loved.

In the third possibility we felt we could not keep up the charade, and I left, invented a divorce, went back to being a woman again and eventually re-met and married Avigdor, whom I still loved.

And so I go through my daily routine, and I have friends and I have work and I do much the same things as everyone else, and I am still waiting for that final dream. When I dream the last dream, then I will know what to do.

Nell Gwynne,
with Cardigan

You're going to be good tonight.

You are going to be amazing.

You are going to be fucking marvellous.

I know what you're thinking. The old cow's going to give us her usual boring, fucking pep talk. Groan, groan, mutter, mutter, why doesn't she bloody well leave us alone, why doesn't she just let us get on with it.

I'll let you get on with it. When I've finished with you. You know what you are, don't you? A load of fucking geniuses. My little geniuses. I don't know how you do it, really. You make me sick, sometimes, you know that? Because you're geniuses, you make me sick, right? How's that for paradox. You're all shit scared, aren't you? At this very moment you're all quaking, nervous, fidgety. A load of shitless geniuses. Fine thing, that. You can see the headlines tomorrow, can't you? 'Some fine, but shitless performances from our newest theatre company.' That's what they'll call us: a new theatre company. Joke, eh. Twenty years of work and you're still new to some people. Well, I suppose that's always bound to be the case. There's always some unlucky sod hasn't heard of us, seen us.

I want you lot to give a performance like you've never done before. I want you to be so hyped up that you won't be able to wait to get out of your dressing-rooms, even before your call has come over the tannoy – posh, we've got tannoy now, folks – even before you spark with sweaty aggro backstage, waiting for your cue. And by the time you've finished with that little lot out there they'll be eating out of your hand – or whatever other part of your anatomy you care to offer them. You will make them laugh and you will make them cry and you will make them sing and you will make them suffer and you will make them love you and you will make them hate you. And at the end, they'll shout and clap and cheer and stamp and do everything they possibly can to stop you getting out of your sweaty finery and cleaning your face and going home to the tick of your alarm clock.

By the way, Mary sends her apologies. She's got that goddam flu, and cried because she didn't want to miss the first night in our new theatre but there was no way I was going to let her stagger out with a temperature of a hundred and four. Mavis will prompt from the Prompt side, of course – posh, we got a Prompt side now – and I'll kill any one of you who has any need for her whatsoever. And that's not any licence for Mavis to take her eyes off the book for half a second. Anyway, Mary's sorry.

Who'd have thought it. Tannoy. Prompt. Little light bulbs over the dressing room mirrors. A real theatre. Ours. A moment to savour.

Remember when we first saw it? Dark and empty and lonely. I love an old theatre. Crying out for sound and light and warmth. Reminded me of that barn we used to rehearse in, just outside Bootle. Bloody freezing. One forty-watt light bulb. We used to call it 'Hell's Waiting Room'. Outdoor bog. Stank to high heaven. All of us constipated for days because we couldn't bear to use it. From such places is magic manufactured. Or perhaps I mean 'in such places'. I don't know. I'm no writer. You know what I mean. In such places we learned to sweat in front of open furnaces at steel works. In such places we discovered what it was like to lose our stomachs as we hurtled down to the coal face in a miner's cage, in such places we were ship-wrecked and seasick, and every time we were our own heroes and heroines and saved ourselves from disaster to travel another day.

I loved that barn in Bootle. That's where transformation took place. And that's why I love an old, sad theatre, like this was. Crying out for transformation. Paint peeling off the damp walls, fraying red plush coming away from seats hanging off their hinges, dust on the box office shelves, mice in the lavatories and spiders all over the lighting board. Sights like that tell me there's a job to be done.

And now look at it. Gilt on the ceiling. Sparkling glass chandeliers. Real glass, no pyrex rubbish. Full, thick, rich paint on the walls. A warm cream. Like smooth, light custard. The sort with no lumps, homely and warming in front of the fire at teatime. Red velvet curtains. Fresh paint backstage, and Andrex in the lavatories.

I know what you're thinking. She's losing her marbles. But a building is alive and responsive and breathes and is warm, or it is hostile and cold and shuts you out. Just like a person can be stripped down and rebuilt and redecorated until they become unrecognisable even to themselves. That's the business we're in. Transformation.

Do not, however, allow yourselves to imagine for one nth of a second that I am growing sloppy in my old age. It isn't sentiment I'm after. It's passion. Guts. Feeling. A hundred per cent commitment. And then some. I don't want the old days back. Giving notes by candlelight because we didn't have a shilling for the meter. Fishpaste and sausages. Broken biscuits and chips. Forget it. Only the rich think chilblains are romantic.

There are, however, things about the old days which will always be with me. And this is where it gets a bit serious, and this is where you start looking away from me, and suddenly you're aware that your left foot is a bit stiff, and you've got this itch between your shoulder blades which is driving you crazy. But you're going to listen, because it is the great British failing, not listening. And getting uncomfortable when someone rabbits on about beliefs, principles, ideas. Didactic, they say, as though didactic was a sink full of greasy dishes. Political, they say, by which they merely mean that glimpse in the mirror you get the morning after the night before, when you turn away quickly because you don't like what you've seen. Forget didactic. Forget political. Just listen to the words and think about the feeling, and with a bit of luck you might be able to recall what we all had together, all those years, sleeping in draughty church halls, dragging caravans around and trying to live like snails with our houses on our backs. We're not too old for the odd ideal. The occasional vision.

When I went to drama school one of the first things someone said to me was that theatre was enshrined in words on a page. That our duty as 'actors' – you notice, I trust, that I never use the word 'actors', I always say 'performers', since actors is what men are, and actresses is what women are, and I want a word that means what both are – anyway, where was I. Yes. Words on a page. One kind of theatre. What stays in print. Well, I fought against that, because I believed that theatre was made by people in spaces, with audiences. Theatre had to touch people, be about ordinary people, give them a great night out. I was not at all interested in stuffed-shirt theatre. And I mean 'shirt' in this instance, and not blouse, because it is men who make most of our decisions, and not women. As usual, I'm trying to say too many things at the same time. Simplify, pare it down. That's what I say to you. Practise what I preach.

Right. So on the road. But I'll tell you a little secret. Although I have become known – a legend, even in my own time – for bringing to life a newly popular theatre, look back on what I actually did. I toured Shakespeare when it was oh-so-unfashionable and bourgeois on the left to do Shakespeare. Dead, moribund, bourgeois poetry. Dozy arseholes. *Measure for Measure* in – yes, in Bootle. Went down like a tornado. When I toured plays and shows which dramatised the class struggles of the day, which took ordinary people's experiences and dressed them up and celebrated them onstage, then the dinner jackets and the fur coats sneered at me, and said I wasn't doing real, serious theatre. If you have an ideal, you don't fit in. And if you work your guts out for your ideal, no one thanks you for it. However wise and cynical I may be, as I get more and more grey hairs, I still, somewhere in the innocent bit of me, I still want everyone to pat me on the back, approve of what I've done, tell me how clever I am. Oh, shit. Now I am getting maudlin. Maybe I'll jolt us all out of it. Do a Laban movement class, right here, with all of you all dressed up. No. Not a good idea.

Me apart. Put me to one side. History. We are a part of history. We've come a long way into history. You've humoured me. Even those of you who left the company in a rage, swearing I was a sadist who liked to destroy people just for kicks. Hours and hours of slog and improvising and meticulously rehearsed spontaneity, creating a moving show, illusion upon illusion, until even you believed that what you were doing was spontaneous. No compromise. I'm no great intellectual. But I'm a thinker. And I'm a doer. And I make other people do. If they won't do, they can fuck off.

By the way, I'm going to keep a close eye on the tableau at the end of Act One. I might want to shift it to the beginning of Act Two tomorrow, which will mean changing the last monologue in Act One. If I can't get the bloody writer on the blower, we'll do it tomorrow morning.

I don't usually talk about myself. I don't expect you've ever heard me talk about myself. Not really. Know why? Because she wears her heart on her sleeve. Because – apart from the odd trip abroad with an American oil magnate – she hasn't got any personal life. All her passion and emotion go into her theatre. Well, a fat fucking lot you know. I don't talk about myself because there hasn't been a script written that gives me the words. Because I'm a woman. Oh, Gawd, she's gone from the pompous to the sentimental and now she's moving on to the obvious. But think about it.

If someone said to you, what's she like to work with – you'd have used all sorts of phrases and things, but I doubt very much whether you'd have made a point of the fact that I'm a woman. What could you have said? She's an exception to the rule that women don't make great theatre directors; she's rather ugly and dresses badly. She swears like a fucking trooper. She's loud. She's not very feminine. She's not very motherly. She's not very sexy. But I bet you wouldn't have said any of those things because you wouldn't want to admit you'd even thought them. Because I have wrought the ultimate illusion upon you all. You think I'm one of the boys. I'm no Antigone, whose devotion to her brother excludes all thought of her independent interests. I'm no Lady Macbeth who goes mad with the frustration of being the power behind the throne. I am no virgin Joan of Arc who is strong and heroic and leads armies, but dies in a suitably poignant fashion because she has transgressed her given gender role. Gender role. That's something I've picked up from these newer young women in the theatre. You see, I will not be a martyr to my cause. Whatever I do will be because I have decided to do it, and because it fits into history. And to that extent I have pulled the wool over your eyes. I do pass as one of the boys.

I don't want to talk about that any more. About myself. My childhood. Where I came from. Orphanage. That's about it really. No curiosity about my parents. Bastards. Whoever they are. Would you give your child away? Not on. I'm not interested in extenuating circumstances. Forget it. Anyone who's a parent of mine has got to make a lot of retribution before they come anywhere near me. Perhaps that's why I'm so keen to get into history, to live in the present, and to live for the future. Never thought of that before. Interesting.

But I'm not introspective. Doesn't interest me. You know what I'd like to have done? I'd like to have lived a hundred years ago. I'd like to have worn huge floppy bloomers, and bought myself one of them old, heavy, iron bicycles – well, they wouldn't have been old then, they'd have been new – and then bicycled my way round Europe. I'd have been an adventuress. An eccentric British adventuress. A hundred years ago, if you had the guts – and the money, I suppose – you could bluff and brave your way through the shit and the flak, and you could go against the grain, and there would have been a category, a word for you: eccentric. And, of course, you would be even more way out on a limb if you were eccentric – and a woman.

There. I'm back to it again. Don't seem to be able to keep away from the fact. I am a woman. Simple fact.

You know what the trouble is? No one in this country likes difference. The class system, they say? Oh, no, my dear, that's long over, long gone. We no longer have class differences any more. Everyone can talk posh like what I do, if they really try hard. No more class in Britain. Sex warfare? Oh no, just the law of nature, little frisson of antagonism makes the game all the more exciting. Anyway, darling, the sexes are equal now. Women have got the vote. Women are liberated. Ha ha. Like a nice liberated woman, myself. Wouldn't want my son to marry one, though. Race? You mean the Welsh and the Scots? Oh no. Those other – chappies. The ones who live in South London, Toxteth. That sort of thingy. Race Relations Act, eh? Takes care of all that. All over, these silly little divisive social categories. All the fault of those trendy sociologists in the sixties. Makes me spit.

You iron out difference, and culture is dead. You pretend there is such a thing as uniformity, you're lying. Common interests, absolutely. Uniformity, forget it. And when I say 'different', I don't mean 'different and unequal'. I mean something like 'different and equal'. And that, you can bet your little eyeliner, is what those at the top don't like. What, working-class men, women, blacks, able to create a culture they control? A theatre in which they decide what they want to do? Why, that's a ghetto. We don't want a ghetto. We want one big happy family. And we know who's the fucking Daddy in that big happy family.

By the way, there's a pigeon that's nested in the fire

bucket on the Prompt side. Mavis, I don't want you throwing chewing gum wrappers in there. And for Christ's sake, don't anyone chuck cigarette butts, lighted or not, into that bucket. That's one non-smoking pigeon, and even pigeons have rights in my theatre.

My theatre. I do think of it as my theatre. I shouldn't, I know. But I do. I feel like Miss Annie Elizabeth Fredericka Horniman must have felt up in Manchester. I feel like Lady Gregory must have felt in the Abbey Theatre in Dublin. I feel like Joan Littlewood must have felt at the Theatre Royal. I feel like Eliza Vestris must have felt, when she stopped showing her legs onstage, put on a long dress and turned theatre manager. Strange, isn't it. How all the important managerial ladies in theatre history have dressed funny. Look at me. Nell Gwynne in a cardigan.

That, of course, is it. When I want to know who is influencing me to influence you – I think of Grimaldi. I think of Hetty King. I think of the Commedia dell'Arte. But when I want to know who I am, I think of Miss Annie Elizabeth Fredericka Horniman, I think of Lady Gregory, I think of Eliza Vestris and I think of Lilian Baylis. All dressed funny.

And by the way, any of you deviates from what we decided finally this morning gets their arse in a sling. A little billet-doux from me tomorrow morning, written in block capitals, I promise you, in red Pentel, stuck on the notice board for everyone and their dog to read. Lilian Baylis once had to get an understudy to go and play Juliet in the play of the same name, *Romeo and*. Understudy feels her little heart pant-panting, sees a star is born in every newspaper, tele appearances on chat shows, Michael Parkinson creaming his knickers, understudy goes out under the lights, comes back off into the dark, and old Lilian says, 'Well, dear, you've had your chance and you've fucked it.' Never let that be said of you. Never. This company doesn't have understudies. You can never have an understudy. When you've fucked it, you've fucked it. As the gynaecologist says to the woman in labour, 'The show must go on.' Only some of you will get that joke. Never mind. It'll grow on you. Anyone who doesn't understand it come and ask me after the show. Come to think of it, anyone who doesn't understand it might as well not bother.

We've got our theatre. Where we wanted it. In the middle of a city, where lots of people live and work. Smart and light and beautiful and comfortable, and people will come and drink in the bar, even when they don't want to see the show. You never know, the show might be a critical success. It might transfer to the West End.

That made you sit up. Hear me say the words 'West End' without sneering at the old bags in their fur coats, the fat ignorant critics snoring over their little writing pads, the trendy paunches in their grey suits, the little nippy radicals in their jeans and leather jock straps. Well. What has happened to the old bat? Where have her principles gone? It doesn't frighten me any more, because I can take it or leave it. There's a lot to be said for getting a show like this on in the West End. There are all those people who never go out from one year's end to the next, who might book up on a charabanc coach trip for a matinee. It might even get on television. I got no time for television, but there's lots that have. If it doesn't get destroyed by those anguished pricks who call themselves producers, that is. There. That please you? A bit of the old spark still there.

My quest is over. You know what a quest is, don't you? Someone wants something, and they set out on a journey, and on the way they have many adventures. In the end, if they are heroic – which really means if they are a brave and handsome young man – if they are heroic, and can survive suffering and hardship, they achieve their goal and get their reward – which is usually the princess who's been sitting quietly somewhere embroidering in her tower. Well, I've gone out for my Holy Grail, my people's theatre, and when I haven't found it already there, I've made the theatre and gone out to find the people. The people, you see, are always there. Some of them will even squeeze their way in here, properly dressed for a night out, not wearing the downbeat

of the trendy scruff, or the crumpled grey pinstripe. They
will have a shave and do the bouffant hairstyle and make
sure their seams are straight. They know how to treat a
theatre with respect. So I went off and quested for a popular
theatre, and I didn't find it, so I made it, and it found me
my audiences. Goal attained. End of quest. I don't have to
scrounge for plywood offcuts to make sets out of, scour
second-hand clothes shops for stuff to make over into
costumes, oil the treadle sewing machine I picked up off a
scrap heap. I've seen a lot of the present and a little bit into
the future and I know it works.

I'm sorry I was late for the run-through this morning. I
hate lateness.

There's going to be a party after the show, onstage. And
no one, but no one is to piss in the flowerpots, no matter
how wasted they get. Mary got a case of Chianti yesterday.

A few weeks ago I got this script through the post. Well,
people send me scripts all the time. I wouldn't have enough
time to read them if I did nothing else all day. So I don't
look at many. For some reason I looked at this one. Quite
short. Two-hander. For two women. I started reading and I
couldn't stop. I didn't want to throw all the pages in the air
and see what came down in improvisation. I wanted to see
it just as it was. In fact, I began to wonder whether I ever
wanted to see it on stage. Oh, it was a play all right. It
didn't need a word to be different. It was quite complete.
Written by G. R. Smith. Well. Smith. I didn't believe
that, for some reason. Doesn't really matter what the play is
about. There was something in the writing of it that got
me, somewhere in the centre.

This morning she comes to see me. The writer. Out of
the blue. Following up her script, she says. In her experience
theatres are total bastards about reading scripts at all, let
alone reading them properly. So when she does bother to
send a script, she often follows it up in person. What do you
think, she says. You've read it. She's young. Well, about
forty, I suppose. That's young from where I stand. She has
dark hair, grey peppering the dark, looks rather good,

actually, made me glad I'd never bothered to dye mine, and she looks nervous. No make-up. Wide, wide eyes. She looks as if she could be beautiful. Sod it. She is beautiful. She says, will you produce my play. I look at her. I shake my head. She says, why, don't you like it. I say it's brilliant. So, she says, what's the problem. Me, I say. I'm leaving the theatre.

Oh God, she says. You can't leave the theatre. What will we do without you? Do without me, I say. I'm beginning to be amused. The theatre has managed perfectly well without me for thousands of years, it will no doubt limp on quite well when I've gone. But you are unique, she says, no one has done work quite like yours, everyone speaks of you — As a legend? I say. I suppose so, she says. After all, how many women have managed to help change the course of history of one of the arts. Bullshit, I say. It's only a small corner of the world. Besides, look at it this way: over three hundred performers have passed through this company, and heaven knows how many other people have had some involvement with a show at one time or another. Everyone takes a little of that experience with them. I am not important. But you are, you are, she says. You really are unique.

Well, I say, thanks for helping me to see it. What, she says? The reason why I am leaving the theatre, I say. I don't want to be unique, I don't want to be on my own, out on a limb, a token, a freak token. I don't want to be used as currency in other people's lives. I don't want people to use me as an excuse not to pioneer their own thing. Then she looked at me very carefully. You're lying, she said. You love being unique and the only one, you are an arrogant cow, really, you're afraid you might be past it. I nearly threw her out of the building.

But I didn't. She's probably crazy with frustrated artistic sensibilities, I thought, you know what dozy flowers these playwrights are. I made some coffee. We didn't say a word while I was making it. When I sat down again, we both raised our mugs in a silent toast to something or other.

Then I said: right in one. I am an arrogant cow. I am a powerful woman. I make things happen. I have got myself the reputation of the filthiest mouth this side of the Comedie Française. I have lied for my beliefs. If I need to, I will tell whatever lie is needed to make something happen. I am praised and feared. People would give their lives to work with me. People would die rather than work with me again. That's it, she said. You are a living legend. That's it, I said. I have entered history. *Ergo sum*. I can relax.

Well, she says, what about my play. What about your play? Who will do it? I don't know, I say. The odds are high that it won't get done. It's too good. The text is too tight. It doesn't allow a half-arsed director to get in there and patronise you. You demand and you challenge. The trouble with the theatre is that it is riddled with mediocrity. Mediocrity rises like scum in this world. You can skim it off the top, like it was a pot of soup, but more will appear and bubble to the surface, leaving a grey slimy mark. And at this the woman gets up and shakes my hand. Perhaps I'd better write a novel, she says. Oh no, I say. You can always write a novel. Women have written goddam novels for centuries. But women only write plays at certain moments in history – well, they are only *seen* to write plays at certain moments in history. Get it done, even if you have to direct it yourself. And don't change a word of it. As a director who has changed every single word of a script when she thought it was necessary, I know what I'm talking about.

Then she goes. And I realise I'm late for the run-through. I look for the script, to see if she's left her name and address on it. But I can't find the script. Perhaps she took it with her. But she was nowhere near my desk. And she didn't have a bag to put it into. So I went in for the run-through and gave you a bollocking because you were so fucking diabolical.

By the way, there's just twiglets tonight. I don't want any of you getting crisps trodden into the carpet after the show. So no crisps. Just twiglets.

I told you Mary sends her apologies, didn't I?

One more thing I want to say. There was a village we played about ten years ago, somewhere in the Home Counties. God knows what we were doing in the Home Counties. Not exactly the bastion of working-class popular culture. Anyway, we played in the village hall – it was *The Caucasian Chalk Circle*, I think. Culture to the middle-class philistines, that's what it must have been. Anyhow, we went to the pub afterwards. Remember the pub? In the snug, there she was, charcoal grey three-piece suit, pageboy haircut, high wing collar, cigar in her mouth. Efficient, very friendly, peaches and cream, low-cut blouse, her bra strap kept showing and she kept pushing it back under the frill. After closing time, I left my hat in there, so I knocked on the back door, got no answer, so I just went in, and they were sitting at the table in the room at the back, having a cup of coffee, no cigar, and they were sitting on opposite sides of the table, and it was quite quiet, and the suit's right hand was on the table, and the blouse's left hand was on the table, and they were holding hands on the table. Very quiet and affectionate. And I stood there in the doorway, and they both turned and smiled at me, and I grinned back, and they went on holding hands. I said, sorry to barge in, but I think I left my hat here. No trouble, said she in the suit, and got up and took the hat off a beer barrel and gave it to me. They're both still smiling. And, out of impulse, I hugged both of them. Just like that. Hugged them both, very smooth and quick, and they both hugged me back. And as you know, I must be about the only one in the bloody theatre who doesn't go round hugging and kissing everyone. In my book when someone calls you 'love' or 'darling' in the theatre, you're in trouble.

Well, that's all it was. A little incident. After that show finished, you remember I went off for a holiday with this American oil magnate who'd been following us around, admiring our work. Well, it was said I went on holiday with him. Mary came too, of course. And the American oil magnate was only interested in our work. A generous man. When he admired something, he was generous.

By the way, Mary is leaving with me.

I suppose that's just about it. I expect some of you will be shifting in your seats, swapping secret snide looks, having a bit of a snigger, saying well, what do you expect, she's not very feminine, she's not very sexy, she had a miserable childhood, she never learned how to make the best of herself. Well, you don't know how wrong you are. Some of you younger ones – feminists, perhaps – will want to jump up and down, claim me for your own, a pioneer with alternative sexual tendencies. In a few years, when I've got a bit of distance on all this, you can come round and have a drink, and I'll tell it like it was. But I'm not one of you. Nothing has come easy to me. Not my theatre, not Mary. The barricades are still up, and I have to settle for being eccentric, dressing funny. But you can include me in your history, if you like.

And now, that's quite enough time-wasting. No more fucking bullshit. There's work to do. You may have heard noises from the props cupboard. Well, it isn't mice. It's a lion cub. There's a lion cub locked up in the props cupboard. It's a very hungry lion cub. It's been kept away from its mother. It's very fond of its mother. Normally it will leap around its mother for hours, and sometimes it sits curled up by its mother and it kneads at her with its sharp little claws. It's not a very happy lion cub at the moment. Its little teeth are very sharp. Its little claws can already rip. Any one of you fuckers forgets so much as the teensiest pause, slips up on timing, leaves out a comma, any one of you takes any notice of me when I nip onstage and join you for the final chorus, any of that, any hint of any of that, and you get the lion cub set on you. And that's a promise.

Tonight you are going to be fucking marvellous.

Breaking and Entering

She had been exhilarated by Joan Littlewood's Theatre Workshop at Stratford East, she had strained eyes and ears to hear the beauty of Shakespeare from the top gallery of the Old Vic (remember when they did the complete cycle of plays over about five years?), she had watched Wesker, admired Arden, enjoyed Jellicoe and delighted in Delaney. Now she was finally grown up, the theatre was the place for her, she thought. But what to do. Actress? Writer? Director? She paced the floor, decided on one, then changed her mind and went for the other – and finally she gave up, drank her Ovaltine and made for the Land of Nod.

In the early blue hours of morning she was woken by a figure. It wore a flowing white gown and before its face it held two masks, one smiling, the other frowning – you know, those masks which are meant to represent the theatre and its two facets, Comedy and Tragedy. The figure reminded her vaguely of a definition she had once heard about something in history happening twice, the first time as tragedy, the second time as farce – or was it the other way round? Anyway, there was no time to get it sorted out because the figure was nudging her.

'What's going on?' she asked.

'Want to see your future?' asked the figure.

'You bet,' she said eagerly.

'Come on then,' it said, 'follow me and I will show you your future.'

Well, it seemed a bit weird, someone breaking into her house in the middle of the night and offering to tell her fortune, but what the hell.

'What's your name?' she asked the figure. 'Mine is –'

'I need no labels,' interrupted the figure. 'I have no name, I have no identification, not of race, nor class, nor sex. I am the Muse.'

'But you must have a name,' she insisted.

'My name doesn't matter. Now, don't waste any more time. Let's go.'

There was something about the way the figure spoke which made her feel as if she was in the middle of an action-packed television series, so she grabbed her candle-wick dressing gown and followed the Muse out into the street. The Muse strode off ahead of her.

'Hey,' she called, 'wait for me. My feet aren't as big as yours.'

The Muse stopped while she caught up, and she noticed that they were standing by a poster. On the poster were two photographs of the same woman. In one photograph she was dressed as Lady Macbeth, and in the other she was wearing a sort of Playboy Bunny costume.

'How about that,' said the Muse. 'You could be an actress. There are lots of good parts for women. Or should I say lots of women have good parts? Joke? Good parts. Women. Get it?'

'Oh, yes, I get it,' she said. 'But I'm not sure about being an actress. You see, I'd be out of work far more often than any of my actor friends – when I say actor, you understand I mean the male of the species – and when I was in work, my average earnings would be lower than those of any of my actor friends. Unless I was a star, that is, and there isn't much room for many of those. The competition is fearful.'

'That's true,' said the Muse. 'You've got to be very good indeed to survive in this business.'

'I thought of joining one of the big companies. But when I inquired about it, I found out that they only take a small proportion of women compared to men. Why is that?'

'I suppose it's just the way the historical cookie crumbles,' said the Muse. 'Great plays simply don't have many parts for women in them. That's just the way it is.'

'How interesting,' she said. 'Do you mean that great plays are only about men and not about women?'

The Muse laughed. 'You've got a lot to learn, my dear. Great Plays are about People and Great Issues, not about men or women.'

'But isn't it true – to corrupt something which Elizabeth Barrett Browning says in her verse novel, *Aurora Leigh* – "Poets must needs be men or women". – plays must be about men or women or even both.'

The Muse patted her on the shoulder. 'You read too much, my dear. I'm sure Elizabeth Barrett Browning didn't mean anything of the kind. She was married to a great poet, you know.'

She was just about to take the Muse up on that when they were interrupted by a group of figures running along the pavement, wearing top hats, cloaks lined with pound notes, clanking saucepans tied around their hats.

'Who on earth are they?' she asked.

'Hooligans,' said the Muse. 'Bad-mannered, spoilt spongers who make a lot of noise. Now look, why don't you become a designer. Girls like making clothes, don't they, making rooms look nice. Wouldn't you like that? I bet you're good with your hands.'

'I don't know,' she said. 'It's very skilled work, isn't it? I don't think I'd be very good at it. Oh, look. I'd love to have a go at that.' And she pointed to where a group of men were welding, sawing, hammering something.

'Dear me, no. That's very rough work,' said the Muse. 'Spoil your nail varnish, that would.'

Some large and heavy object flew over their heads.

'What on earth was that?' she asked.

'That was a two-hundredweight flat,' said the Muse. 'We've got this wonderful new crane that can lift heavy objects. Marvellous thing, machinery.'

'Then I could learn to operate the machine, couldn't I,' she began.

The Muse patted her on the head. 'Very, very difficult, my dear. It's not a sewing machine, you know.'

Now a procession of people pushed them off the pavement. They were carrying billboards and posters, advertising a Women's Theatre Festival. She was most intrigued by this, and turned to follow them, but the Muse was tugging her sleeve. 'You don't want to bother with them,' said the Muse, 'they're just a load of amateurs, or at best lousy professionals who can't get work. Come and look at this. I've found the very thing for you. Here.'

The Muse was standing by a table with lots of white envelopes on it.

'Now,' said the Muse, 'this is the perfect job for you. It's just as glamorous as being an actress, but far more responsible. You need a good telephone manner, neat hair and make-up, smart, sexy clothes, but nothing too low-cut. On first nights you can dress up and meet all the important gentlemen critics. There you are. Publicity.'

'I think I'd prefer to be one of the critics getting their tickets in one of those nice little envelopes,' she said.

'Out of the question,' said the Muse. 'Far too many women muscling in on that already. You wouldn't like being a critic. It's far too responsible a job. Arbiter of taste for the public. No, no, not at all suitable for a woman.'

They were walking along a corridor with many rooms opening off it. From the rooms came the sound of music, dancing, talking. The Muse opened one door and then closed it very quickly, but she just had time to notice that the room was full of women wearing leotards or funny clothes, somersaulting, clowning and generally being extremely athletic. 'That looks exciting,' she said.

'Must be some sort of therapy group,' said the Muse.

'Builds up the muscles in a most unattractive way.'

The Muse opened another door. Inside were two circles of people sitting on chairs. In the middle of one circle stood a man, in the middle of the other stood a woman. The Muse beckoned her inside the room and they stood watching.

'Now observe this,' said the Muse. 'Look at him. Strong, yet sensitive; passionate, yet creative; intelligent, yet in touch with the concerns of the common man. One of our foremost directors. Now look at her. No authority. Loses her temper. Unfeminine. Difficult to work with. She won't make it as a director, I'm afraid. Hasn't got the stamina. Besides, as soon as she starts up the ladder she'll piss off to have a baby. Can't take the pace.' And the Muse ushered her out of the room.

From behind a half-open door she saw a group of people: ten men and two women, rehearsing a play. They watched for a moment. 'Look at that,' said the Muse. 'Perfect balance. Strength and a little light relief.'

Through another half-open door they saw another group rehearsing, this time five women and two men. 'Ridiculous,' said the Muse. 'A totally unbalanced cast.'

'What is it?' she asked.

'They call it "positive discrimination",' said the Muse with a sniff. 'Rubbish, I call it. Just an excuse to stop talented actors getting work.'

She stood still. 'I think I'll try my hand at writing a play,' she said.

The Muse stopped short. 'You can't be serious. I mean, apart from Aphra Behn and Lilian Hellman, oh yes, and perhaps Caryl Churchill, there are no women playwrights.'

'Well, you've just named three,' she said.

'But they're not great playwrights. I mean, where is your Shakespeare, your Congreve, your Ibsen, your –'

'I would like to write more parts for women,' she said.

'There are great parts for women already: Antigone, Medea, that boring Phaedra woman, Cleopatra – oh, the list is endless.'

But the Muse saw that the idea would not go away, so

they wandered into a coffee bar and sat down, and the Muse began again.

'Look, if you're serious about writing a play, let me give you some expert advice. First of all, make sure it has lots of action. Now we all know that men are the active, and women the passive sex, so it stands to reason that most of your important characters must be men. If you insist on writing about women, okay, make your central character a woman, but make sure she is surrounded by lots of men, and if at all possible, either kill her off, or make her go mad. That is essential. Now if you have too many scenes in which women talk to each other, scenes without men in them, that is, you will be told that there's not enough action and that the characters do not develop. Remember, women only develop in relation to men, and that is as true in art as it is in life. If you possibly can, just write a little light sit-com; after all, you don't want anyone saying you haven't got a sense of humour, do you? Don't be too heavy or solemn. Women can't write about important issues, so don't even try. Women are only interested in the domestic and the trivial. When women love they are sentimental, when men love they are passionate. When women fight for a cause they are foolhardy, when men fight they are heroic. Your best bet is to write a play which has as its central character an anguished, middle-class male on the verge of the menopause; but I doubt whether you'll be able to do that because it is a well-known fact that women can't write about men. If however, you still insist on writing about women, make sure they're sexy, played as comedy and take their clothes off. That way you may stand a chance.'

'But wouldn't it be a good idea if more women wrote plays?' she asked.

'No, no. We can't watch the theatre going to the dogs while women write mediocre plays.'

'I've seen lots of mediocre plays by men,' she said lightly.

'Have you?' said the Muse offhandedly. 'Now look, we had a play by a woman on in the West End last year. Isn't that good enough for you?'

'No,' she said. 'Anyway, it wasn't a very good play.'

'Bitchy, bitchy,' said the Muse. 'Running down our sisters now, are we? Women always scratch each other's eyes out in the end.'

'Wasn't there a festival or something a while ago?' she asked. 'It was called something like Women Live, and went on for a month.'

'Oh yes,' said the Muse. 'Jolly good idea, that. Let the girls have their say for one month and then they'll shut up for the other eleven. Beano wheeze, that was.'

She looked up at the Muse. She realised that the voice coming from behind the masks was quite posh. On impulse she reached up and grabbed at the masks. Behind them was the perfectly nice, friendly face of a man.

'At last,' she said. 'Nice to see who I'm talking to.'

'Rumbled me then, have you?' he said.

'There's nothing to be ashamed of,' she said. 'You should face up to the fact that you're a man.'

'I'm not ashamed of it,' he said gruffly. 'I just feel safer behind the masks. Oh well. Now you've rumbled me I suppose there's not much point giving you any more advice. You won't take any notice of me anyway, will you?'

'No,' she said. 'I won't. But I'll still remember everything you've said. Sorry, but there it is.'

'You're going to go into the ghetto, then?' asked the Muse.

'The ghetto?' she asked.

'Just working with members of the one sex,' he said.

'Certainly not,' she said sharply. 'I wouldn't dream of being the only woman working with a load of men. I want to work with other women, and some men, and have choice.'

'Sounds a bit abstract,' he said.

'It's very simple. I just want to do what you men have been doing for centuries: work with members of my own sex when I want to.'

'Oh dear. That won't be at all popular with the men who run the theatres.'

'That's right,' she said. 'It won't be popular, but it'll be terribly good for us. It might even be good for you if you keep your eyes and ears open.'

As she finished her sentence she noticed that the Muse was becoming fainter and fainter in outline. She waved until he was out of sight. Then a ringing filled her ears. She turned round to find her alarm clock blazing away. She switched it off, got out of bed to go and sit at her typewriter. She found she was already wearing her candlewick dressing-gown.

He did not want to compose another *Quixote* – which is easy – but *the Quixote itself*. Needless to say, he never contemplated a mechanical transcription of the original; he did not propose to copy it. His admirable intention was to produce a few pages which would coincide – word for word and line for line – with those of Miguel de Cervantes . . .

Cervantes' text and Menard's are verbally identical, but the second is almost infinitely richer. (More ambiguous, his detractors will say, but ambiguity is richness.)

'Pierre Menard, Author of the Quixote',
Jorge Luis Borges.
(*Labyrinths*, Penguin, 1981)

Grace before Dinner

Green beans, haricots verts, flageolini: slim, rounded bodies, a hard stubby end where they were once attached to the plant, a tapering fine tail, slim as a tadpole.

She holds a bunch of the beans in her left hand, flexes her fingers gently to get the tops evenly in line with one another, then, with a deft cut of the silver-steel Swiss army knife, she cuts the stubby ends off. She likes the cool green feel of the beans; she likes the serene delicate touch of the sharp blade, she likes the way the knife fits neatly into her palm. She always uses this knife for delicate operations in the kitchen.

As she tops and tails the beans – there are a lot of light beans in half a pound – she remembers the sharpness of the air that autumn morning: the little shop in Old Compton Street in Soho which imports fresh French vegetables. The wheezy old lady who served her, moving slowly between the scales and the shallow wooden box which held the beans in their white tissue paper. At the back of the shop, the tall old man moving slowly and silently, stooped, like some kind of craggy runner bean.

As she rinses the beans under the cold tap and puts them into the red cast-iron saucepan, she remembers the walk to the

*Algerian shop to buy coffee beans, the walk to the market in
Berwick Street to buy new potatoes, Spanish onions, lemons,
a crisp Webbs lettuce, a pound of small, sweet continental
cucumbers. Then the extravagance of a taxi across to Notting
Hill, to her favourite butcher's, to buy a lean dusky pork fillet.*

*She puts a shallow layer of water in the saucepan, adds a dab
of butter, grinds some fresh black pepper, some coarse sea salt.
Then she puts the lid on the saucepan, and places the saucepan
on one of the back burners of the electric stove. Though in many
ways a rather chaotic person, she has a neat, methodical
approach to cooking, and every move, dove-tailing with every
other move, is cherished.*

One

I first met Grace sometime in the middle of the 1970s,
1975 I think it was. A group of us, friends who worked in
journalism, publishing, one or two in fringe theatre – sort
of intelligent, vaguely radical people about the media, I
suppose – used to meet on a Sunday afternoon once a
month; each of us would bring something to read, an
extract from a novel, a poem, anything at all really which
we might have come across or dug up, or liked. A sort of
offering to one another. It was very relaxed and easy-going;
in the few months that I had been going I had been
surprised at the lack of competitiveness, the way people
listened to one another, showed interest, sometimes caught
enthusiasm for a particular writer; we would read for about
an hour, then whoever was hosting the event would serve
tea and cakes and biscuits, we'd all chat and then we'd all
go home. It was a mildly literary interlude, which we all
enjoyed.

The Sunday Grace first came was a bright autumn day; a
few brown leaves flying round the streets, but not yet the
damp, clinging setting-in of winter. In keeping with the
weather I wore a long flowing kaftan with sequins and bits
of mirror sewn into the fabric – the sort of thing that was a
bit out of fashion, but which was comfortable and made me
feel I was as seamless and flowing as the fabric.

Out of the corner of my eye; a new face, blonde hair cut in a heavy pageboy shape which swung round her chin. Grace. She was smoking little roll-ups, and looking down at the ground. Then, as I began reading my offerings, she looked up, and I felt the focus of a sharp gaze on me. When I finished, I looked up, and caught sight of her bright, still, blue eyes. We smiled at one another. I had read a passage from D. H. Lawrence's *Women in Love*, and a poem by an obscure Latin-American poet, whose book I'd picked up in a second-hand shop in King's Cross.

When tea was brought in, and everyone was milling around, Grace bounced up to me and introduced herself. She really enjoyed what I'd read, and hadn't she seen me somewhere recently? A conference on local housing, perhaps, or was it the premiere of a film about an American feminist painter?

Those, I said, were my two outings over the previous fortnight. What a coincidence, she smiled – how wonderful. What did I mean, 'outings'? Oh, I said, I was wrestling with some work at home, and hadn't been going out much. The two outings were events I was covering for the local newspaper, which kept me in bread and butter. What work at home, she asked? Oh, just this silly novel I've been writing, I dismissed. Novel, she said, her eyes shining – how wonderful; a real writer. I knew you were a real writer, the moment I heard you read. I looked directly at her for the first time. She was smiling, her right hand held the small cigarette, her right elbow was held crooked in the palm of her left hand; she was wearing jeans and a floppy sweater, no make-up, her face alive and concentrating utterly on me. I had a sudden desire to talk about my novel, to tell her the plot, to describe how hard I found it to stick at it, and yet how much I wanted to finish it. I wanted to read her the pages, I wanted to give her the words and ask her what she thought, wanted to have her approval, her enthusiasm. It was an odd feeling. I couldn't quite understand it, and so I looked away, and made a joke about real writers being writers who published something every year. Oh, she said, I

103

had already published something, then? Just a short novel, I said, juvenilia, young girl runs away from home to join commune – that sort of thing. I'm sure it's not juvenilia, she encouraged. Where can I buy it? Out of print for years, I said. Then I'll get it from the library, tomorrow, she announced.

Then my friend Arthur came over to us. Well, the word 'friend' is really the only reasonably neutral one I can think of to describe him. We had a very intense affair a few years ago, just after my novel was published, and then settled for friendship, and what was now a very real affection. I introduced Arthur to Grace, and they shook hands, and then somehow that special aura which I felt had surrounded Grace and me dissipated, and it was just a room full of people saying goodbye after Sunday tea.

She takes the pork fillet out of its rustling polythene bag; she takes a large, sharp kitchen knife and slices the fillet lengthways, into four flat strips. She lays the pork escalopes into a broad, shallow pyrex dish, and then mixes a marinade; dry martini, lemon juice, salt and pepper. She pours the marinade over the pork fillets, turning them over so that they are moist on both sides. She covers the dish.

Two

The following month Grace came to the group again. The weather had turned chilly, and I was wearing my jeans and a shirt and sweater. Grace was wearing a long, flowing Indian cotton skirt, and an equally flowing cotton top. Over her shoulders she wore a shawl. She had curled her hair, and it looked a little untidy. This time she had brought some pieces to read. She read a poem by D. H. Lawrence and an extract from a novel by a little-known Mexican woman writer – she had found the latter, she said, in a secondhand bookshop in Ealing. When she finished reading, there was a little silence in the room. This was quite usual; a mark of respect, and also a moment in which everyone could digest what they'd heard; sometimes we would go on to the next reader, sometimes someone might ask a question or make a comment. But this time, there was a little flurry of spontaneous applause – something I didn't remember ever happening before. I felt mildly irritable – envious in some way, I suppose, although I could not really think why.

The moment passed, and again Grace bounced up to me during tea, asking solicitously how the novel was going. Again, her face was open, direct, her body relaxed, standing very near me, her interest concentrated and genuine. I had had a good week and was feeling optimistic. She was delighted, hugged me and said how pleased she was for me. As her arms went round me for those few seconds I had a pang of remorse for having felt so irritated at the applause she'd got. Out of a desire to expiate my tiny guilt, I said how much I'd enjoyed the pieces she'd read. Oh, I'm so glad, she said; I do love discovering obscure writers. It's my magpie thing, she said, I just can't help it. Actually, she said – she hoped it wasn't impertinent of her – but she'd really like to talk to me some time, if I wasn't too busy, that is, she knew how precious my time was but – oh, of course, I said, I'd love to.

She takes the brown paper bag of potatoes, and tips them out on the draining board, in a flurry of fine dry earth. Some of the potatoes fall into the stainless steel sink, rolling around like dirty marbles until they come to rest in the middle. She turns the cold water tap on, full and hard, a fine aerated jet coming straight onto the potatoes. With her fingers she rubs the gritty surface of the potatoes, savouring the squeaky smoothness as each slides, grit-free, in her hand under the water. Into a plain cast-iron saucepan she puts the clean potatoes, unpeeled, covering them with water. She stands this saucepan beside the beans, on the other back burner.

Three

A few days later Grace phoned me up. I got your phone number from Arthur, she said. I was sure I remembered writing my number down for her on Sunday, but I didn't say anything, because she was bubbling with the suggestion that we should meet for supper. A new crêperie which had just opened in Notting Hill, just round the corner from the flat she'd borrowed from a friend.

We met that evening. Round wooden tables, candles on the tables, a casual sort of clientele, an easy-going atmosphere, French posters on the walls. We floated through two bottles of Chianti Classico (red), and seemed to talk intently and non-stop. It was so easy. She told me about herself. She had left home when she was seventeen, refused to take up her place at university, because she thought it was a waste of time. She'd spent the last few years living in squats, in communes, now and again with a man. She worked some-times in a pre-school nursery, she liked children, but didn't think she wanted to have any. She really wanted to be a writer, like me, a real writer and she thought that children would interfere with that. She felt that feminism was really important because it gave women our voices back, and she thought it was really important that we should all become aware of that. What did I think? Of course I agreed, but I found it hard to agree; that sounds a bit topsy-turvy; what I mean is that she was so enthusiastic, her eyes shining so much with the remark, as if she had really discovered it for the first time in the world for herself, that I felt the desire to say that of course I felt that, she knew I was a feminist, there really wasn't anything staggeringly new about that remark, the question really was, how did we do it, what did we think of our task? But I choked back the cynicism that I felt would erupt, because she was so comfortably contained within her warm moment of discovery, and the candles were shining, and the wine was warm, and the crêpes were luscious and savoury. So I merely agreed. Then she asked me about myself. And that's when the strange thing happened.

I found myself, by imperceptible degrees, with the greatest of ease, and with a flowing sense of release, a sense of having found the right time and place, telling her about the novel I was working on. In great detail. And she listened, and nodded and smiled, and ordered more wine, and filled my glass, and was pleased, and laughed and approved and – I had never had such an audience. I had never talked about my work that way before. Even to Arthur, who had often been the recipient of moans and confidences. But he had never listened in precisely that way. He had never made me feel, through his eyes, the way his body leaned towards me, that I was without doubt the most important and interesting person in the world at that moment. And I had never talked about the relationship between my own – soul, for want of a better word – and my fiction. I told Grace how the subject of my novel, a fantasia about the life of a seventeenth-century Spanish nun, was in a way a metaphor for all sorts of things about myself which I could not come to terms with: faith, spirituality, devotion. My voice had never been so subtly heard.

As we were drinking our coffee, which she had ordered without my noticing, I realised I had been talking non-stop for an hour. I apologised. She dismissed the apology with a wave of her cigarette. I said, My God, you must take a full hour of my time, Grace – it wasn't fair of me. Well, she said, her eyes looking away, her fingers fidgeting with a box of matches, there is something you could do – but no, I won't ask, you have so much important work to do. No, no, I said, what is it, what can I do for you. Well, she said, I've written a story. Great, I said – and absolutely meant it – no pang of irritation or envy here at all. Would you – I mean, might you have time just to look at it and tell me what you think? You can be quite honest about it, tell me if it's rubbish. Of course, I said, I'd love to read it, and if I can be useful, then I'd like that.

Grace took out of her shoulder bag a scroll of paper, rolled up and held with an elastic band. Only if you promise to tell me what you really think, she said. I promise, I answered, and I meant it.

Outside, with the wine and trust inside me, I was heady with the ease with which we had found such friendship. When she embraced me to say goodnight, I kissed her on the cheek. In reply she kissed me on the mouth, not a sexual kiss at all, just a wordless contact, a soft promise of trust. Next time you must come round to my flat, she said, and I'll cook for you. I love cooking.

The outer leaves of the Webbs lettuce have stained the paper bag dark brown. She detaches the outer leaves carefully, pinching off the brown edges and rinsing each leaf carefully under a gentle jet from the cold tap, then placing each leaf into a red enamel colander. She takes care when handling the leaves, so as not to crack the translucent leaf in its curve. She places each leaf in the colander with the rounded part of the leaf upwards, to make sure all the water drains away. As she gets further and further into the heart of the lettuce, she has to be more and more careful with the tightly packed leaves, so as not to break them. Finally, she reaches such a tight clutch of yellow-white leaves, that she decides not to peel any more and she bites through the heart, relishing its crisp sweetness.

Four

As soon as I walked home, my head whirling, I went into the kitchen, made a cup of coffee, and sat down to read Grace's story. I could tell, even through the alcoholic haze, that she had some literary ability, a kind of flowing, sensuous style. The story was awkwardly constructed, and felt a little as if it had been written in a great rush, and then not re-read carefully enough. I got a pencil and found myself marking bits that needed looking at, suggesting a way to re-arrange the beginning, cutting a bit from the end. It took me an hour or so, and when I'd finished I had an impulse to ring her up, tell her what I thought, get some response from her, repay her in some constructive way for the friendship she had shown me. I realised then that I had forgotten to get her phone number. Nor, I realised stupidly, did I even know her surname, and so could not look her up in the phone book. I wasn't terribly worried, really, just a bit disappointed not to have been able to give way to spontaneity. I went to bed, after first heaping some books on her manuscript, to straighten the edges which were still curving up, after having been rolled in the elastic band. Not a bad first effort, I thought, about a young girl, living in a hippie commune.

She begins to mix a dressing for the salad; a feast of gentle, unflowering colours. First, green-tinged olive oil from a large green and silver can, bought in a Greek delicatessen. Then half a lemon squeezed by hand directly into the oil, parts of the pulp going in, the pips lifted out with a spoon. Then a peeled garlic clove, a luscious clove, fat and opaque, imported from Provence. Then some mustard, already made with mustard seeds and vinegar. A pinch of brown sugar, fresh pepper and salt. She whips the mixture with a fork until it is cloudy, with tiny bubbles in it. Then she dips her right forefinger in, tastes it, and relishes the mixture of sweet, sour and tart tastes.

Five

I rang Arthur the following day, to see if he knew anything more about Grace's whereabouts than I did. As soon as I mentioned her name he exploded on the phone. That ball-breaker, he yelled. I was astounded. It wasn't usually like Arthur to use language like that, especially in the hearing of a feminist friend. When he'd simmered down, he explained: they had been having a fraught and tortured and very passionate affair since the first Sunday meeting. I couldn't entirely understand why it had been so fraught, but it had something to do with Grace vowing undying devotion to him, being very passionate and loving, and then not turning up when they'd arranged to meet, or forgetting to do something she'd promised. He'd get angry, she'd be very contrite – she always had a good reason; the word he kept using of her was unreliable. And to cap it all, he said, they had been talking about going away for a week, and last night she'd come round to his flat very late and told him she was going to Canada for six months.

Arthur was so distraught, that I comforted him as best I could, arranged to meet him for a drink, and advised him to try not to let it get him down too much. I didn't like to ask for Grace's number – it would have felt like adding insult to injury somehow. So I rang off and went out to do some shopping, feeling very confused. Why hadn't she told me she was having an affair? Well, why should she? I answered myself. Because, I countered, I had talked at great length to her about Arthur, and it was just a bit odd that she hadn't said anything. Why hadn't she told me she was going to Canada? Why should she? Well, because – because – no, true, why should she. Oh, because from the way we'd talked the previous evening I had somehow got the impression that this was only the first of many evenings where closeness and intimacy and shared interests would make the occasion sweet.

In W. H. Smith's I bought a handful of magazines to leaf through. When I got home, I sat down at the kitchen table to check through, read articles, look at stories, see what was around being written by and for women. There was the usual range – from very conventional cookery and beauty articles, to the more speedy and upmarket magazines aimed at the working woman, and the woman who aimed at urban sophistication, being in with the cultural swim. In one of the latter magazines, to which I had sold a couple of stories in the past, was a story heralding, it said, a 'major new talent', a story by L. Grace Newman. Well, I thought, Grace is a common enough name. I turned to the page, and there, in a rakish inset at the top of the page, was Grace looking at me, trusting, intimate and smiling. I gripped the magazine. I read the story through. I compared it with the flattened scroll of words. It was the same story, with a number of adjustments, very similar to the editorial suggestions I had marked in pencil the night before.

When I put down the magazine and the manuscript, my hands were white from tension. Grace must have known the story was being published – indeed, it must have been out yesterday when we met. Or at any rate – well, she could not *not* have known.

I didn't know what to think. I didn't know whom to talk

to. On impulse I went to the phone, then stopped. I realised that in some weird double-thinking way I had wanted to ring up Grace herself, and ask her what she thought about it all. Then I remembered that I didn't have her phone number, and that jolted me into realising that I couldn't possibly talk to her about it. What could I say? I had no claims on her. We scarcely knew one another. And yet the day before I felt she was my oldest and best and dearest friend. It was too much of a muddle. I did no more work that day. I decided that I was probably exaggerating my reactions, and maybe I'd get some clue at the next Sunday gathering.

She peels away the outer layer of an onion; her eyes smart as she cuts into the root, and a milky white liquid oozes out. She holds the onion under running water, blinking fiercely. The water dilutes the white juice and her eyes stop smarting. She takes the onion in her hand, and with the Swiss army knife criss-crosses the onion, making what looks like a grid for a multiple noughts and crosses game. She slices horizontally across the onion, so that the pieces come away in small, translucent squares. The onion is piled on a plate.

Six

Grace wasn't at the next Sunday meeting, of course. As the days passed, my turbulence at seeing the story she'd given me in manuscript, already in print, faded. It was probably a silly coincidence. Perhaps she'd been shy about admitting it was going to be published. Perhaps I'd mis-understood what she said. After all, we'd been quite drunk. So what if she hadn't told me about Arthur. So what if the theme of her story was the same as my first novel. I didn't have a monopoly on juvenilia. All the so-whats helped the sharpness of the confusion fade. The intensity of the promise of a new friendship also faded, as my life began to change. I continued to work on my novel, slowly, and almost pleasurably. I also began to do some teaching, literature courses, and some creative writing sessions. I enjoyed these a lot. After I'd been doing the classes for a few months, I found I was spending less and less time on my novel. Every so often I would look at the pile of neat pages, and feel a pang of guilt, but mostly I was so busy that the guilt didn't last. Then, one day, after a particularly successful class, I found myself suggesting that we should continue to meet outside the classes, and perhaps start a more serious writing group. Some of the students were keen, and with a couple of other women friends, we began meeting. It worked rather like the old Sunday meetings, except that this time we read our own work, discussed, commented and criticised. It was very stimulating, and exciting.

She puts a tablespoonful of olive oil into a deep frying pan, adds a tablespoonful of butter, and when it is hot, adds the onion squares. While they fry gently, she takes the pork fillets out of the marinade, dips them on both sides in seasoned flour and when the onions are transparent, she puts the fillets in the pan to brown. Then she adds the marinade and a little water to the pan, stirs it, turns the burner down low, puts a lid on the pan and leaves it to simmer. Then she pours herself a glass of dry Martini, adding ice and a slice of lemon.

Seven

A year passed very quickly. My new group had a break for the summer and then met again in the autumn. We had a kind of party at the first session, and on a wave of euphoria someone suggested we should publish some of the writing we'd done the previous year. This provoked a lot of discussion – why publish – why not – was it good enough – would anyone be interested – why write if not to communicate to others – what about the ego, yes, what about the ego – but the upshot was that we decided to continue meeting, and try and put together the best of our work into some sort of book or pamphlet. That was to be this year's project.

After the party, I took out my novel, and looked at it for the first time for weeks, finding a new surge of energy, and resolving to finish it. I had just sat down at the typewriter, when the phone rang. A smiling voice greeted me with, Oh, how lovely to hear your voice. I thought it was the wrong number, when the voice enthused, it's Grace, remember me, God, it's been ages, how have you been, I've been dying to have one of our good old chats – no, I'm on my way to see my parents in Leeds, I'll phone as soon as I get back in a few days, take care of yourself and I'll see you really soon.

When I hung up, I went back to my desk, but the pages seemed flat, the words mere markings on the page. I had forgotten what effect her voice had on me. Largely, I was delighted and pleased; I realised I was smiling, tidying the flat up. I had a vague niggle of annoyance – why no word all this time – but that was all dispelled at the thought of seeing her in a few days. I put my novel back in its drawer, and I no longer felt guilty about it.

Carrying her second Martini, she takes the cheeses out of the fridge: a triangle of Brie, gently springy to the touch, a small Boursin, creamy with garlic and herbs, a wedge of Emmenthal, dry and oily, with odd-angled holes. She puts all the cheeses on a board, covers them with a clean tea-towel. She takes some water biscuits out of a packet and arranges them on a plate.

Eight

Of course I didn't hear from Grace. I should have known. Gradually, as the days passed, I began to feel a sort of leaden disappointment inside me; I realised as I went about my daily routines that I had been looking forward to telling Grace all about the year during which we hadn't seen one another, about the teaching, the writing – somehow I felt that my time would only fall into focus if I could present it to her for her approval or her enthusiasm. The leaden feeling grew as each day passed, and I became aware that my readiness to slot into a wonderful conversation was being slowly numbed. Quite inexplicably, I told myself, in the occasional moment of rationality. But, I would remind

myself, what about her promises? Oh yes? What promises?
And that I couldn't really answer. A good conversation –
the unrequited desire for a good conversation couldn't
possibly explain the depth of depression I had sunk into.

A few weeks after the phone call, I got an invitation to a
book launch. Arthur was working for a large and respectable
publisher, and every now and again he would send me
invitations to book launches. I never went, feeling awkward
and shy and – yes, envious. This time, however, the
invitation was mysterious; it announced the launch of the
autumn list of novels – five altogether, and promised to be a
'vibrant literary occasion'. Arthur knew how depressed I
was, though he didn't know why (I didn't really know why
myself) and on the day of the party he cajoled and coaxed
me into believing that I might enjoy it. So I went.

*She tidies the small sitting-room, heaping the cushions on the
couch. She moves her large leather armchair, so that it stands at
right angles to one end of the couch. She goes to her desk, and
takes out a blue file. Then, re-filling her glass, she goes to the
leather chair, sits in it, opens the file and slowly reads over the
ten pages of typescript which are in the file. She smiles with
satisfaction.*

Nine

I dressed carefully, wearing a neat skirt and shirt, low
heels, and no flamboyant colours. I thought that if there
wasn't anyone there I knew, then at least I'd be an unobtrusive wallflower. The event was held in a large London
hotel, in a room festooned with flowers and book jackets.
I didn't really notice much more than a blur of colour, since
I was too busy looking round to see if there were any
familiar faces. Then a figure ran towards me, dressed in a
brightly coloured, flowing Indian kaftan, embraced me,
kissed me on the cheek and said how pleased she was I
could come, the occasion wouldn't be complete without
me. Grace grasped my hand and took me across the room to
a table where Arthur was standing with some other men all

dressed, it appeared, in the same kind of grey suit. In among them Grace looked bright and delicate, like an exotic and beautiful jungle bird.

She took a book and put it in my hands. Here it is, she said. Look inside it. I opened the shiny cover, and there, on the acknowledgements page, was a dedication to me, for all the help and support I had given Grace. Then she introduced me to the men; Arthur looked pleased, we smiled, I shook hands with them all, Grace taking great care to tell them I was her very best friend and I was a very important writer. I was so flattered by this that I forgot my fury that Arthur hadn't forewarned me.

I spent the rest of the evening munching canapes, sipping wine and chatting inanely. Somehow I felt I couldn't go home, couldn't leave, even though there was no explicit stricture on me to stay. Grace was busy talking to any and everyone, and at one point she was the centre of a group of journalists, all of them taking notes busily, as she held forth, her cigarette held high and casual in her right hand; she looked confident and vulnerable at the same time. When people began to trickle away, I slipped out, still clutching the book. I got home, and – fully aware that I was in the middle of a kind of *déjà vu*, I sat down and opened the book. I speed-read my way through the prose, almost knowing what I would find, and yet gripped and fascinated, daring myself to be disproved, continually shocked as I was not disproved. The novel was a rather deftly written fantasia about the life of a seventeenth-century nun, a kind of extended metaphor for some of the existential tussles facing a woman today: faith, spirituality, devotion. It was the most extraordinary experience; it was not simply that the subject was so identical with the subject of my unfinished novel, it was that I felt deeply familiar with the tone, the questing, curious, desiring tone of the whole thing. Here was my novel and yet not my novel; it was powerful; even if I could have categorically seen it as plagiarism, I could not deny that it stood up absolutely in its own right. And the book was dedicated to me. That in a way was the most puzzling thing of all. Did Grace deliberately – what – steal, take, be inspired by – whatever word you like – me, my thoughts, my work, my being. Or was she simply the trusting innocent she appeared, absolutely meaning every kind and generous gesture, quite unaware of the effect she might have on people? And how on earth could I decide? And when I had decided, what would I do? What could I do?

She lays the table: red paper serviettes, wine glasses, bread plates, knives and forks, a bunch of autumn flowers from the window box in a small vase in the centre of the table. In the kitchen the pork fillets are still simmering gently. She breaks the lettuce leaves into a bowl, sprinkles some darker, feathery dill leaves over the lettuce, and takes the bowl and puts it on the table. Then she goes into the bedroom, and carefully changes into a brightly coloured flowing cotton kaftan.

Ten

A couple of days after the book launch I got a hastily scrawled note from Grace. She had been madly busy, and just wanted to let me know that she was going to Australia to do a year's writer in residence, a terribly exciting thing, and she was planning to get a writers' group going there, all women, and perhaps they would publish some kind of book of their work. She would do her level best to see me for a drink before she went.

I smiled when I read the note. I knew I wouldn't see her, and indeed I didn't. I also smiled when I read about the projected writers' group. Grace's bright, smiling face had been seen all over newspapers and television programmes, talking at great length about her voice as a writer, and everything in the note was already familiar to me from interviews she had given other people. Except, of course, the bit about wanting to see me.

Grace was away for a year again; during the course of that year I found myself absolutely unable to finish my novel. I kept writing endings and ripping them up. At one point I decided to rewrite the whole thing from the beginning, but

I found I couldn't. By the time Grace contacted me again, I'd almost forgotten what it felt like to write something and be pleased with it. In a way it bothered me; but at another level I felt freed from anxiety – I couldn't entirely explain why. It was as though, now I no longer felt caught up in an agony of tension, fear and creativity – would I like what I wrote, would I finish what I was writing, would it be good, would it be published – now I could relax, do my teaching, enjoy my friends, read books, and be quite a contented, relatively anonymous person.

Then yesterday morning the phone rang. It was Grace, a little gushing, her voice sounding a little bit forced. When I asked her how Australia had been, she sounded abstracted, and said very little, just that it had been hard work, a bit lonely, and she thought she'd been having a writer's block. But she really needed to talk to me, she said. She had felt so out of touch. I heard my voice saying, easily and brightly, come round and have supper here tomorrow night. Grace's voice broke into relief, could she really, that would be marvellous, that was just what she needed, some wise advice from someone. But wouldn't it be a bother for me? No, no, not at all, I'd cook, no trouble. Come round about eight.

The rest of yesterday was extraordinary. It was one of my working at home days, when I had no teaching. After Grace's phone call, I sat down at the typewriter, and with a sense of total self-assurance, I typed and typed. Not any kind of re-hash of the novel, no new ending or new beginning – well, no, actually, a new beginning was exactly what it was. I had not pre-planned it, but in the hours I worked yesterday, I produced the first chapter of a new novel: a story set just before the outbreak of World War One, in a small seaside town whose desultory pace is entirely overturned by the war. I knew I might have to polish the odd sentence here and there, but I also knew that the chapter was right, that although I had no clear idea of precisely where the story would go, or even who all the characters were, it didn't matter. The novel was there and ready. I put the chapter into a new file, and put the file into my desk drawer. Since I live alone, normally I never lock anything; but for some reason, I fished out the key to the drawer of the desk, locked the drawer with the chapter in it, and then put the key into the cutlery drawer in the kitchen. Then today – well, I've told you most of what I did today.

At eight-fifteen, the doorbell rings. She puts down her glass, goes to the door and opens it. She stands for a moment, smiling at her guest. Then she embraces her, kisses her and says, 'Come in, Grace. How nice to see you.'

Eleven

The meal was delicious. I was really pleased with myself. Grace clearly enjoyed it, settling into my large armchair as if it were her own. Although I had tried to be meticulous about my preparation for the meal, I had somehow forgotten to get wine. But that didn't matter. Grace had brought a bottle of Muscadet, a perfect match with the dinner – almost as if she had known what I would be cooking.

We chatted and gossiped; who was doing what, where, with or without whom. Grace talked about living so far away from her friends, where she hardly knew anyone, where she wasn't at all famous. She had missed me especially. You could have written to me, I said. Oh, I'm hopeless at writing letters, she said. But not at writing other things, I probed, genuinely curious, not at all cutting, really.

She leaned forward, her brow creased. It was awful, she said. Just awful. She had been unable to write a thing in Australia. Oh, I said, surely there must be something that's salvageable out of a year's writing. No, you don't understand, she said. I literally did not write a word. I used to sit down with my notebook, or in front of my typewriter, and I could not get the letters to appear. She couldn't understand what on earth had happened. She had never had that kind of – well, writer's block before. Could I explain it.

I couldn't, of course. To distract her a little, I began

talking about our writers' group; I suggested that perhaps Grace might like to come to that. Oh no, she said, I couldn't possibly. I need my own vision, something which just comes inside my own head. I don't think I would know how to function in a group like that. But I'm being selfish, she went on. What about you? Well, I said, I hadn't done much the past year. Busy, yes, but not produced a lot. Suddenly she was out of her chair, sitting on the floor beside me, her hands clasped on my knees.

I don't know how to explain this, she said, but when I was in Australia, I was miserable the whole time. Then, as I was getting on the plane to come back, I suddenly realised that I needed to talk to you. That was it: you're so wise and experienced about writing, you know so much more than me, you understand things so much better. Oh, that's silly, I said, I'm no wiser than anyone else, really. But you are, she insisted. I'm absolutely sure of that now. What do you mean, I asked.

She sat back on her heels. Well, she said, after I phoned you yesterday, she said, after I heard your voice, the minute I got off the phone, I had this idea for a novel. It's a novel about war, set probably just before World War One. What do you think? Do you think women can write novels about war? I'm sure we can, I said. She jumped up and began pacing round the room, all her old energy back, talking, not very coherently, but about how wonderful it would be to get back to being able to write again, and how grateful she was to me for somehow making this possible. I suggested coffee, and she agreed to that enthusiastically.

I went into the kitchen to make the coffee and, opening the cutlery drawer to get some teaspoons, I caught sight of the red Swiss army knife. Without thinking about it, I took the knife and slipped it into my kaftan pocket. As I ground the coffee, put it into the percolator, I felt a strong, surging determination to finish my new novel. I went back to the cutlery drawer, took out the key to my desk and put that in my pocket with the Swiss army knife.

When I took the coffee into the living room, Grace was

once more sitting in the large armchair. She was leaning back, her eyes closed. She looked a little tired. I noticed some fine lines round her eyes. I put the tray down on the coffee table, and stood behind the chair. My right hand went into my pocket, and I felt the Swiss army knife. I took it out, and played with the blades. I took a slim blade out. Then with my left hand I stroked Grace's hair. It was soft, and very slightly wavy. Mmm, she said, that's nice. I smoothed the hair away from her right ear. The skin was soft and smooth. Mmm, she said, that's lovely. I feel as though you're taking away all the worry, so that my head's quite free, quite empty.

The Swiss army knife had a delicate feel to it; it fitted snugly into the palm of my hand. The blade slid easily through the soft whorls of Grace's outer ear. Then it met resistance, bone, a flash second of pain. Not long, because I worked quickly and deftly; my left hand was clamped over her mouth, pressing her head back against the chair. Really, it was no more than a fleet split second. She did not suffer. I could tell. Then she relaxed, a faint smile still on her face. The hole was round and neat, only a slight grey-pink frothing at its edges. I wiped the blade on my dress, and snapped it back into its red casing. Then I put two fingers of my right hand into the hole. Very slowly and carefully I felt round, then, when my fingers found what they had been looking for, I drew them slowly back out of the hole.

Out came a scroll of tightly furled white paper. Again I put my fingers in, and again out came a scroll of tightly furled paper. Within about five minutes there was a splay of rolls of paper on the coffee table. Finally my fingers met empty space and I knew that was all.

I sat down and began unfurling the papers and reading what was on them. Of course I knew what would be there. It was a short, beautifully written novel, about the First World War and – but you know already what it was about. The first chapter was missing, of course, but that was because I had already written it, because it was in my desk, locked away, and Grace had not yet had access to it. There were some other scrolls of paper, still unopened, but I decided to leave them until later. Who knew what else there might be there – poems, stories, even another novel perhaps. I would use them in the future, as I wished.

I stood and looked at Grace. She really was rather pretty. I was a bit sad; I would miss that heady euphoria of promise which had accompanied her into my presence. I would even miss – a bit – the disappointments when she let me down in tiny ways. But I knew I wouldn't miss the sense of emptiness, the envy, and the difficulty of writing a piece of fiction which was being fought over in an invisible ring, with no rules to keep or break.

I wrote a short letter to Arthur; I flattened the pages of the novel, added my own first chapter, and parcelled the whole lot to be sent off to Arthur in the morning. Then I washed the dishes, tidied up the room and went to bed. I knew Grace would be gone in the morning.

The Interview

He was very beautiful. She had seen him often on
television, and there was no doubt at all that he was
photogenic. She had also occasionally seen him in the
park, where he took his children at weekends. In real life
he was not particularly tall, and looked a little unhealthy, a
little pale. She had read all of his books, and had reviewed
a couple of them for the suburban paper she worked for.
The newspaper's circulation was dropping, and there were
rumours that it might close; she began casting her sights
further afield, exploring the possibilities of going freelance,
of braving the cut-throat world of metropolitan journalism
proper. She made very little personal, direct effort, but did
spend one weekend typing out letters, photocopying some
of her better efforts and sending them off.

She didn't expect any responses really, so it was a surprise
when she got a telephone call from one of the Sunday
newspapers, asking her if she would interview the writer.
The voice at the other end of the phone said that they were
trying out a number of fresh approaches, people who had
not already done the rounds of national newspapers, and
they had chosen half a dozen unknown journalists at

random. Her letter had arrived, they liked her cuttings, so . . . she asked for a couple of days to think it over. Should she, she wondered – indeed, could she – interview someone about whose work she had very mixed feelings, and whom she knew was seen in the literary world as the nearest you could get to a male pin-up. After the requisite couple of days, she realised there was no way she could find out whether or not it was worth doing, other than by doing it. Besides, it was a chance to branch out. Just what she'd been hoping for.

As the days passed before the interview, she brushed up on his writing – novels, biographies and articles – checked out the biographical details, began to think about the kind of questions she would ask him. The evening before the interview, she felt intensely nervous. As a journalistic assignment it was no more difficult or spectacular than anything else she was used to doing. Just before she went to sleep, she realised that she was nervous because he was so beautiful, and she very much wanted to be in the same room as he. She wanted to look at him closely, to have him look at her – and as she thought this thought, she allowed herself to develop it. Perhaps they would strike up an incredible instant rapport, they would plunge headlong into a helter-skelter passionate affair, which would leave them both helpless and ecstatic. A romantic, erotic fantasy, brought to life at the prospect of going to interview a beautiful man. She was quite amused at herself. It was almost as if she had won some prize, and was to be taken out for the evening by a glamorous celebrity. Of course, he was a glamorous celebrity, but there the resemblance between fantasy and reality ended. She was merely a fellow professional who would, as the interviewer, be in control of the event. In the face of such a practical and functional reality, the pitter-patter of a nervous heart could have no place. She slept well.

She took a long time deciding what to wear for the interview: a long, softly-gathered skirt, neat black shoes, plum-coloured tights and a plain, white, long-sleeved shirt.

Efficient, she hoped, and (secretly) perhaps discreetly attractive. She drove to his publisher's office and was shown into the office of his editor. The receptionist told her that the writer was already waiting for her, and as she came into the office, he rose from the leather chair behind the desk, holding his hand out, and saying his name. She took his hand, shook it efficiently, said her own name. Then he offered her a cup of coffee, and when she accepted, already busy taking her coat off, he left the office, leaving her to set up the tape-recorder and assemble her first impressions.

Soft, almond-shaped eyes, deep and still and direct. That must be one of the keys to being photogenic: the ability to look straight and clear into the camera, straight into the soul of the viewer. Such clear eyes, that you felt *seen*, as though the eyes were drawing you easily into their own depths. A pear-shaped jaw, the bones wide, ever so slightly slavonic in shape. A soft lower lip, full and firm, and a soft upper lip, strongly shaped, no cupid's bow, not a gross mouth, a mouth that somehow retained an impression of childlike freshness, with an adult confidence: perhaps together that was the meaning of sensuous. At such close quarters, even though they had only been in the same room for thirty seconds, there was no doubt. He was beautiful. The nose was slightly flattened, contributing to the sense of softness, his face creased gently when he smiled, very white teeth showed even and clear, his hair was cut soft and feathery, falling over his forehead and round his ears. Definitely beautiful.

He came back carrying two cups of coffee. He apologised for having taken so long, saying that he'd been talking to one of the young ladies about publicity for the book. At the phrase 'young lady' she felt a little chill flow round her. A sort of pang of sadness, that he had to use such a conventional cliché, such an apparently chivalrous turn of phrase, but a phrase which carried along with it the reverberations of patronage, superiority, flattery and the sense of her being a member of a slightly inferior cultural group.

As she adjusted the tape-recorder to make sure the built-in microphone was facing him, she recouped her inner composure. How, she thought rapidly to herself, could she have expected him to use phrases other than 'young lady'. After all, just because he was beautiful, it did not follow that he would be radical, or even sensitive to some of the ways women did or did not like being addressed. In any case, this invisible and anonymous 'young lady' was the one who should or should not be offended. She realised that her frisson was on her own behalf; she did not want him to think of her patronisingly as a 'young lady'. She would have to block off the possibility by simply fulfilling her professional function.

She settled back into her chair, holding her coffee, and looking him full in the face for the first time. His eyes were clear and direct, but without any hint of a personal or particular emotion. Just the beauty of his proportions, the warmth of the texture of his features. With the desk between them, they both had distance, and could each choose whether to look at the other, out of a window, at the books on the shelves, or at the chaos on the desk which belonged to neither of them.

She was a very skilled interviewer. She didn't use notes, she didn't have prepared questions. She digested her research, and then relied on the spontaneous material generated between her and the interviewee. He was an equally skilled interviewee, giving relaxed and very full answers to each question. She concentrated entirely on him, looking at him all the time, watching his mood, listening to his answers, sensing when he might be coming to the end of an answer, thinking ahead to the next question, she the pursuer, following his signs, he the pursued, free to look away, in other directions, knowing she would follow him, while she listened, nodded agreement, smiled encouragingly, occasionally interpolated a lightning interruption to indicate that she knew what he was talking about.

She was focussing very intently on his face, and so was aware of the rest of him only out of the corner of her eye. He was wearing a dusty pink shirt, a red and grey striped tie. Unusually for her, she found it difficult to get any clear impression of his hands. Normally she would notice a man's hands as quickly as she registered his face. Some men had beautifully slender fingers, slender wrists, rising to the smooth strength of the forearm, warmed with soft hairs, very different from the slimmer sweep of a woman's forearm. He kept his hands loosely clasped in front of him, and did not seem to need to use them, knowing, perhaps, that it was his face that provided the strongest focus anyway.

As she concentrated on his face, and as he talked, while she listened, she saw herself rise from her chair, go round the desk towards him, lean over and take his face in her hands, one hand on each cheek, cradling his face, tilt his face up towards her, run her fingers over the contours of his face, put her cheek against his, feel the close-shaven smoothness, kiss his face, feel the different softnesses. In this fantasy he did not respond or take any initiative, and she was left to explore his face as and how she wanted. And meanwhile the soft, West Country burr continued, giving him that slight vulnerability which some of his fellow writers lacked, burdened as they were with the hard edges of the urbane public school drawl. While he was in no sense a hard-line radical, his sense of social conscience – the social conscience of the upwardly mobile man, which can, genuinely, if somewhat patronisingly, sympathise with the difficulties of those who have not been so successful in their fight – combined with a refined but definitely non-metropolitan accent, gave him a sense of being accessible to anyone – intelligent, somehow of the people, and yet acceptable to the liberal men of conscience in the media, running our cultural institutions. It also gave him the confidence of his own conviction and an articulacy about safe, liberal concerns. He spoke fast, with a gentle rhythm, soft but not seductive.

There were only two questions which he parried during the interview; parried might even be too strong a word, because he simply responded as though he hadn't heard them, and continued answering the previous question. One was about the relationships between the male characters in his work. Had he been a radical by repute, she might have asked him directly about the homo-erotic nature of these relationships. But she was a little wary of sounding too jargon-bound; so she approached the question indirectly, saying that she found the relationship between the men rather interesting. No flicker, and he simply continued talking. The second question, a little later, was during a brief silence which she filled by asking him how he liked being interviewed. Again, no indication of response, as to whether or not he had heard, and then, when he began speaking again, it was to revert to an earlier comment he had made, to amplify and expand it.

It was, all in all, an extremely professional sixty minutes. She got everything she wanted; she had not expected a complete confessional, she had not even necessarily expected him to say anything he had not said in other interviews. They had efficiently covered a variety of themes, and he had supplied enough biographical information to ensure an intelligent and fluent read.

She looked at her watch, expressed her thanks and began to collect her technology. As she gathered tape-recorder cassette box, pen and pad, he got up from the desk, stretched and loosened his tie. She felt his mind was already elsewhere, that he couldn't wait for her to leave. She thanked him again, and hurried out to the lift, professionally pleased, and personally a little hurt, as though she had somehow been let down. As she got into her car, she became aware that there was a polite, tense little smile on her face. She stuck her tongue out at herself in the car mirror, then shivered involuntarily, as if shrugging aside some sort of unexplained discomfort.

She began transcribing the tape later that day. As she did so she saw that he had been a generous interviewee. The answers were indeed full and intelligent. A good piece of work had been done by all. After a solid hour's typing, she got up to make some coffee. As she went into the hall, she was struck by an unexpected splash of colour on the hall

127

table: a red and grey striped tie. She picked it up, looked at it. It was still knotted, as if someone had merely loosened it and taken it off. She was puzzled. She had no memory of taking it out of her bag when she got home; she certainly couldn't remember picking it up in his office. Anyway, he'd been wearing it. Or had he taken it off. Had he taken it off, put it on the desk, and had she just scooped it into her bag in the hurry to leave. She simply couldn't say.

She made coffee and went back to her desk, carrying the tie, which she placed beside the typewriter. She intended to phone his publisher's about the tie as soon as she had finished transcribing the tape. She switched it on, and gradually, as she listened, she fell again into that mesmerised moment when she imagined herself taking his face in her hands, caressing its contours. By the time she finished listening to his voice and writing his words, she had no desire to do anything about the tie. It looked right there on her desk, a curved shape, resting.

The newspaper was pleased with her piece, and over the following months asked her to do other articles, none of which required the sort of in-depth interviewing she had done with him. The obsessive memory of his face faded, so that when she switched on a late-night chat show, and caught him there as one of the clutch of guests, she was able to look at him almost disinterestedly, as if he were merely an articulate, reasonably attractive stranger. She even felt a little secret amusement at her former self for having been so silly, and grateful that her professionalism had prevented her from making any kind of fool of herself. She went to her desk and took up the tie, put it round her neck and watched the rest of the programme calmly and – as she told herself – maturely.

That Christmas she was invited to the newspaper's party. She wasn't keen on parties, but thought it would be politic to turn up, at least for a little while.

As soon as she arrived, she regretted it; the party was in full swing, crammed with people, the air hazy with cigarette smoke. She drank two glasses of wine in quick succession, and could see no one she knew. Her commissioning editor gave her a quick wave across the room, she smiled tensely and wondered how soon she could leave. She looked at the door to plan her exit as casually as possible, and her stomach jumped. There he was, framed in the doorway, his practised eye cruising round the room, checking everyone out. His eye passed over her and although he gave no outward flicker of recognition, she knew he had noticed her. This was the right time to leave. She put her glass down and slid through the crowd to the door. She went to find the office in which she'd left her coat. As she made for the lift a voice said, 'Leaving already?'

The burr was very familiar. He was leaning against the wall, his eyes focussed intently upon her, a small smile on his face. 'I don't blame you,' he said. 'Dreadful things, parties. I hate them.'

'Why did you come then?' she asked.

'Oh, I always go to them and I always hate them. Do you want a lift somewhere?'

'I've got my car, thanks,' she said.

They walked downstairs together. 'Did you like the interview?' she asked.

'I never read articles about me,' he said. 'But I'm sure it was very good.'

'Oh yes. It was.'

'You're very sure of yourself.'

'So are you.'

'Touché.'

She had an overwhelming desire to take his hand, to snuggle up to him, to put her nose under his ear lobe and smell his aftershave. She giggled. 'It's the cold,' she apologised. 'Or maybe it's the two glasses of wine on an empty stomach.'

'Shall we go and get a coffee?' he suggested.

'I've got a better idea. Come and have coffee at my flat. We can go in convoy.'

They didn't say anything as they got out of their cars. She opened her front door and stood aside for him to precede her. They both stood in the hall for a moment, looking at one another. He smiled. Not a 'personal' sort of smile, just a relaxing of his smooth, soft face.

'Are you offering me tea or coffee?' he asked.

'You can have either. Do you want it now or later?'

'I see,' he noted. 'Is this a pick-up?'

'Certainly not. We've met. We're not strangers. I interviewed you, remember? I know all about you.'

'I don't know anything about you.'

'Do you want to?'

'Oh yes.'

'Then we'll have coffee later. Or tea.'

In the bedroom, they left the light off. They undressed each other, with no words, their bodies and hands and faces familiar and at ease, as if they had known each other for years and were still able to communicate and excite one another. They made love, and didn't talk, and caressed one another and explored, and they were both confident and both considerate. Afterwards they talked a little. Just a kind of functional checking of each other's personal situation. He was separated from his wife, and lived in a flat by the river. She was alone, after a live-in relationship that had lasted a number of years.

Their exchanges had leapt from complete and distant professional formality to the intimacy of unimportant small-talk, and the entire expanse of communication in between was not there, and unnecessary. If it was a one-night stand, she thought, then it was seamless and okay. He probably did this sort of thing all the time. The fantasy which she had carried round in her mind, this phantom desire was now laid to rest, exorcised, fulfilled, satisfied.

She slept very well after he left. She thought no more about him for a couple of weeks, and then he telephoned her. He was to be in London for a meeting, and could he drop in for a drink. He came over, they made everyday small-talk like very old friends, and went to bed like very old friends. Afterwards he rather tentatively asked whether he could visit her every now and then, in just this way. His divorce, he explained, was about to go through – oh, no problems, but he and his wife had agreed that until the divorce was final, neither would go out in public with anyone else. It was a kind of token agreement, that somehow was like a final leave-taking; at least, that's how he understood it. What did she think. It was curious, she thought, before she answered. This was not a man who needed to ask permission for anything he did. This was a man who had an air of soft authority about him, who had no problems dealing with the world, and yet who seemed to be showing a very real sensitivity. She simply smiled agreement. Neither of them discussed the status of the relationship, or affair, or whatever it was.

Their encounters continued on a casual basis; a sort of oasis for both of them. In between his visits, she continued with her work and social life, and sometimes when she was lonely, she would find herself replaying the tape of the interview while she cooked or tidied the flat, simply listening to his voice, holding to herself the memory of the impersonality of that first encounter, listening to his cool and articulate voice, and remembering the warmth and comfort of their contact in bed. Before each visit she kept meaning to mention the puzzle of the tie, but somehow when he arrived, she would forget, and it would no longer seem such a puzzle. She had put the tie in a drawer in her desk, and it simply stayed there. He never mentioned it, and as the months passed, she forgot that it had ever belonged to him.

One day, while she was walking through Covent Garden, she thought she caught sight of him in a restaurant, by the window. She went hurrying over, and then stopped; he was sitting with a woman, quite young, and the two of them were laughing. As she watched, they raised their wine glasses, as if they were drinking a toast. She stood for a moment longer, and then turned and walked away, her stomach leaden.

That evening he telephoned and asked if he could come round. She felt totally relaxed at the sound of his voice and said yes, of course. Then, as she usually did, she tidied the

flat, in preparation for him. As soon as she opened the door
to him, she again felt a tight, leaden weight at her centre.
He noticed when she was cool in response to his kiss and
asked what was wrong. Since their relationship had never
needed to justify itself, since their meetings were only
casual, and conveniently so to both parties, since they only
met in her flat, there was a whole range of things which
had never needed to be perceived or explained or understood.
This security – based on an easy and uncomplicated ignorance
– meant that they were always perfectly frank with one
another – insofar as the very limited circumstances of their
relationship warranted. So she had no nervousness or doubt
in asking him who it was he had been seen having lunch
with. He replied that it was the woman who was in charge
of publicity for his publishers. She remembered their very
first encounter and asked if it was the same 'young lady',
trying hard to put no emphasis or gloss on the phrase. He
couldn't recall, he said, it might be. And what were you
celebrating? she asked. The American rights for the novel
have just been sold, he said, and we were having lunch to
celebrate. Surely it would have been more appropriate to
have lunch with the rights person, she said, again not
putting any gloss onto the question. He snapped and said
he didn't really think it was her concern who he had lunch
with. She replied that she had simply thought there was
something odd about it. He then accused her of being
jealous. She said, yes, she was jealous. She only realised it
this very second, but she was jealous because she would like
to be able to have lunch with him, she would like to be able
to be seen in daylight with him. He shrugged and muttered
something about his wife.

At which she did get angry, and expressed all the
turbulence she had tried to keep out of her earlier remarks.
She thought he was using his wife as an excuse. If he could
be seen in public with a woman who worked for his
publishing company, then he could be seen in public with
her. She wasn't proposing that they fucked in public, for
heaven's sake. He became very withdrawn at that, didn't

look at her, went silent, awkward. She felt she had transgressed terribly, but that there was nothing more she could
do. She touched his face, the soft, smoothly-shaven cheek.
He flinched.

He spoke quietly, his burr almost a mumble: 'I don't
think jealousy has any place in our affair.'

'Nothing seems to have any place in our affair,' she said
bitterly.

'Look, we have a very good arrangement.' His voice was
thick and unclear.

'I'm not sure we do.'

'Well, it doesn't have to continue.'

She felt deeply hurt. 'Is that all you can say? Doesn't it
mean anything to you?'

'Of course it does. But it has to stay as it is. I can't be
seen with you in public.'

'Not ever?'

'I don't know.'

'After the divorce?'

'I don't know.'

'I see.' She felt cold, drained, as if they had been
shouting at one another, as if the room had been filled with
a cacophony of sound. Questions whirled in her mind. Did
he love her, did she love him, why didn't he want to be
seen in public with her, did she really mind, she knew it
could never be serious, why is she so upset, what does she
want him to say. She realised that the fact that he had lied
to her galled most strongly. And she didn't feel there was
any point expending emotional energy on arguing – somehow, outside the warmth of bed, they were still strangers.
They did not know one another in the real world, and so
none of the real world, other people, places, events, could
really impinge on their space. She knew that if she tried to
pursue the matter, something violent and unpredictable
might happen – she didn't know what, but it had something
to do with a pressure that would explode. Her head was
hurting. She put her hand to her forehead. He looked
briefly at her, then looked away. At other times if she had a

headache he would have moved easily and stroked her head, soothed her into relaxation. He did not touch her. His eyes were remote. She dropped her hand, her whole body now weary with exhaustion.

'I've got a terrible headache,' she said, matter of fact.

'Perhaps I'd better go then,' he answered, matter of fact.

Both of them allowed the niceties of this small-talk exchange to serve as their leave-taking. He got his coat, took his briefcase and left. They said goodbye to one another at the door, and then she closed the door on him, went to bed and wept desperately until there were no tears left.

The pattern of her life changed very little indeed. The only difference was that he no longer visited her. She took a few days off, as if she were convalescing from an illness, slept late, shopped. After that, things went back to normal. One day, when she was tidying her desk, she noticed that the red and grey striped tie seemed to have been moved from its drawer. Despite searching quite thoroughly, she couldn't find it. She assumed that he must have taken it with him one day, though she couldn't remember when. During that particular clear-up she also found the cassette of their interview. In a rather distant spirit she put it into the machine and played it through. It was odd – the machine kept stopping, and it was only when she rewound the tape, putting a biro in the centre spiral, that it worked properly. She thought perhaps the tape was old; the quality seemed less good, the voice a little remote, a little blurred.

That night she switched on the television as usual, flitting between channels to see what looked interesting. On one channel she came across a late-night chat show, and there the host was introducing a writer whose novel had just been nominated for one of the big literary prizes of the year. She sat up as he came on, wearing a grey and red striped tie. The host welcomed him, thanked him for coming despite a heavy cold, and they began talking. Something made her get up and switch on the cassette, with the tape of the interview still in. For a while, as she sat watching the television, there were two sets of sound audible, the old interview, and the conversation from the television.

Then, as she sat there unmoving, slowly the sound on the television faded, until she could only hear the tape. She went to adjust the volume. As she turned it up she heard the host's voice, asking a question, then the sound went again. She switched to another channel. The sound was fine. She switched back and sat down again, watching. This time she could hear only the host's comments. After a few minutes the tape snarled up in her cassette machine. As she went to look at it, she heard the host apologising to the audience on behalf of the novelist, saying that perhaps he could return to the show when his voice came back. Applause, which she could hear, and then on to the next guest. As she took the tape out of the machine, she saw that it had snapped.

The following day she read in her newspaper a very brief review of the programme, regretting the novelist's sudden illness: he had been rushed to hospital for an emergency operation on his vocal cords. He had some very mysterious ailment, which they hoped they could cure, but it was very possible that he would not be able to talk again.

She sent him a get-well card in hospital, but decided not to visit him. She wanted to remember him as he had been for her – slightly distant and mesmerising, or very close and very warm, and either way beautiful, and a feast for the eyes.

He was not, in fact, able to speak again.

harmony *n.* State of being harmonious; agreeable effect of apt arrangement of parts; (Mus.) (study of) combination of simultaneous notes to form chords (cf MELODY); sweet or melodious sound (*harmony of the spheres*).

Concise Oxford Dictionary

Rick

In a tiny village somewhere in West Africa, at one time colonised by the French, Rick arrives, with his back pack, his Californian check shirt, his duffle bag, his descant and treble recorders, hell-bent on getting out of mad, loud America.

He has grown up in the sunshine and the sand of the surfing fraternity, always a little thin, a little pale, a little too sensitive, enjoying the sea and the waves, but only first thing in the morning or sometimes at sunset, when the beefies had gone in, having found their girl for the evening.

The only son of parents who never planned to have children, who had lulled themselves into a quiet life in which they found peace and comfort in each other's presence. He worked as a repair man for the telephone company, lucky to have his own van, and used to a silent working day, apart from occasional polite exchanges with strangers.

She, as a school teacher, never teaching children over eight years old, also a stranger to anything other than polite adult conversation in the staffroom, or in the supermarket.

Both of them only children of only children.

When they met they talked quite soon of families, and

they resolved that they would either have no children or a very large family, neither wanting to repeat the loneliness of their own childhood, neither wanting to see their solitary pasts reflected vicariously in the life of a child of theirs.

They discovered a fierce catharsis in telling one another their dreams, in sharing the secret games they had played alone in their childhood, rejected or teased by other children, or ignored because their parents were too busy to play with them. There, in their solitary rooms, unknown to one another, they had read the same books, invented the same worlds, built forests out of discarded matchsticks, made a broken train set stand for the first railroad in America, used their dolls and teddy bears as inventors, magicians, gods. Ethel and Carson found that despite being of opposite sexes, they imagined things in the same way. Both had learned all sorts of self-sufficiency, because that was easier than learning to communicate. So he had taught himself to cook, and she had taught herself the intricacies of electricity. Their love of silence was very important to them both, they agreed. They speculated on the nature of this silence, and agreed they did not know what it was. They didn't know if it was happy or unhappy, just that it *was*, and that it was important. They took silence for granted.

Ethel and Carson met at college, where he was doing electrical engineering and she was majoring in English. They married straight after graduation, Ethel a blushing virgin bride, Carson proud and resplendent in a new suit he had saved up to buy from his vacation job in a local factory, sticking labels on decanters of Californian wine.

For their first few years of marriage they lived in one room, and saved. Their spare time was largely spent working out budgets, drawing up lists of furniture, poring over paint colour charts, thinking about carpets, and planning for their first real home together.

They bought a tumbledown shack near the sea, and then all their spare time was spent sawing and hammering and mixing and painting. The sea was their swimming pool, and they no longer went to the movies, or saw colleagues from work at weekends, because there was always so much work to do, and so much satisfaction to be got in doing the work.

At first they were in complete agreement that they would not begin to think about children until they had a home of their own, then, when they had a home, there was always something to finish off, something else to fix up, and before you knew it, some twenty years had passed and the time was still not right to talk about children. Finally, even the thought of children was no longer there in their minds. Until, that is, Ethel's trusty diaphragm, scrupulously used, and regularly checked, let them down.

When she missed two periods she began to think the menopause was starting rather early, and went to her doctor. The doctor asked her various questions and then suggested having a pregnancy test. Ethel was surprised and said why on earth should she have a pregnancy test?

The doctor was young. She examined Ethel and told her gently that she was pretty sure she was pregnant. Ethel said she couldn't possibly be, yes, she had put on a bit of weight recently, and she was feeling hungrier and lazier than usual, but there was no question of pregnancy, she used her diaphragm regularly. Why, they hadn't decided yet whether to have any children. It must be the menopause, she was sure. She didn't mind, actually, she would be very relieved not to have periods any more – but the doctor interrupted very gently and suggested a pregnancy test just to be sure, it could do no harm. The doctor said she could call to find the result of the test, or come in again next week. Ethel was perfectly happy to come in next week, she was repapering the bathroom this week and she would be sure to forget to call.

So the following week Ethel again sat opposite the young doctor who looked at her with clear blue eyes and said that the test was positive, and that Ethel was definitely pregnant. Ethel didn't know what to say, so she said nothing. She felt numb. The doctor asked her how she felt about it, and

Ethel heard herself asking whether it was safe to have a baby at her age. It's a little risky, said the doctor, but you're fit and well, and with care, there should be no problem at all. Ethel felt as if she had a sore throat and said nothing. I know it's probably a bit of a surprise, perhaps even a bit of a shock – you'll probably need time to get used to the idea. Yes, said Ethel, huskily. Do you want to have it, probed the doctor gently, and Ethel's voice suddenly became clear and strong. Oh yes, she said, oh yes. I don't know what my husband will say, she added.

Well, said the doctor, think about it and come back and see me next week, and then we can work out your ante-natal care. Bring your husband as well if you like.

Ethel gathered her coat, smiled at the doctor, said thank you, her voice husky once more, and went out. Behind her the doctor looked at the closing door and then for some reason found tears welling up in her eyes and she put her head down on her arms and wept. Then she blew her nose on a Kleenex and buzzed her receptionist to send in the next patient.

At home Ethel and Carson took the diaphragm and held it up to the light, stretching the rubber gently. There was a tell-tale pin hole. There, said Ethel, it wasn't magic after all. Carson took the diaphragm and ripped it apart, then he threw it in the garbage can and they both laughed. They did not discuss it any more. They began planning, making lists, such as they had for the new stone patio, and for the hand-carved kitchen dresser.

They discussed the practicalities, colours, the crib, the buggy, the room – but they never talked about how they felt about the prospect. Ethel was frightened of the actual birth itself; Carson was terrified at the idea of a wild, wordless creature suddenly appearing into the lives they had managed to order through the practical use of words. He was afraid of how he would feel when it cried. He and Ethel were both afraid they would not love the child, that they did not know how to love the child, and each was afraid to tell the other.

They were, therefore, both entirely taken by surprise at the joy of the birth, at its concentration, at the wordlessness of the labour and its achievement. They were unprepared for the joy they felt when they first saw the little, red, screwed-up face of their son. They both burst out laughing and the baby burst out crying and there was a wordless happiness.

And so Rick grew up in a totally loving, but largely silent household. He did not speak sentences until he went to school at the age of five. Doctors thought he was backward, or perhaps even deaf, and he was put through a series of tests which he accomplished smiling, always showing great intelligence and quickness, as long as he did not have to make conversation. The doctors concluded that his IQ was high despite his being slow to speak. There was nothing wrong with his larynx. It could only be a matter of time.

Ethel and Carson had picked up an old piano at an auction in the early days of their marriage, thinking it might be a nice idea to play. But they had both been too busy, and so the piano had remained, tuned and polished, as a centrepiece of the living room. Until Rick began to crawl and climb, that is. He climbed onto the piano stool one day and began playing with the keys. At first Ethel was about to rush and stop him, afraid he might fall off the stool or damage the piano, but then she saw that he was sitting solid and stable and that he was actually picking out a nursery rhyme tune on the piano with his little fat fingers. This first little exploration lasted half an hour, then he got bored and tumbled off.

From then on Ethel had no fear about leaving him alone in the living room, where he might play with plugs, or break ornaments. He made straight for the piano and would play happily there for hours. Ethel could hear him from anywhere in the rest of the house and so she knew he was safe. He never created chaos round him anyway, he rarely cried, and Ethel and Carson always knew from the slightest sound or indication or gesture what he wanted.

At school he began to speak sentences; he learned to

read and write. He played tambourines and triangles and one day the teacher brought in a clutch of descant recorders which the school had acquired. They were plastic Japanese instruments. The children pounced on them and began blowing in a cacophony of sound, harsh, shrill, wild. Rick took one and went into a corner, put his fingers on the holes, working out what went where and felt most comfortable, and then he blew into it, gently, then more firmly as he felt the way his breath produced the sound. Then he found that by using his tongue against the bit in his mouth he could define the beginning and ends of the notes and he began experimenting, controlling the column of air with his tongue and his breathing, and producing an altogether different tone from any of the other children.

From then on he abandoned the piano and spent long hours with the recorder, playing the music he was given in school, but mostly playing in his room, a sweet, solitary sound. Soon his teacher got him a treble recorder, and he began playing this too. The teacher knew nothing of the music he made at home. He played in the school orchestra, and occasionally was given solos. Ethel and Carson enjoyed the sounds, never thought of it as other than a matter of fact, did not suggest lessons, other instruments. And Rick never asked for anything more than he had.

In this way the years passed. When Rick left his first school, there was no longer a recorder orchestra, and his music continued alone, at home, in his room. He was quiet, unobtrusive, made no friends and no enemies. He went on to college, and one day he got a message to go to see his tutor.

The tutor's face was solemn. He had bad news. There had been a fire. Rick's parents – the house was burnt down. The tutor watched Rick's face anxiously. He did not like having to break news like this. Rick looked calm. He knew what had happened. The tutor did not need to spell it out. Rick did not cry. He went home, arranged the funeral, told his parents' work mates, who all came, were sympathetic but unsure what to say to this strange, unmoving boy.

There was insurance, of course, but Rick had no heart to rebuild the house. He sold the land, put all the money in the bank, and then prepared to return to college. He was about to catch the Greyhound bus, when he realised he didn't want to go back. He realised he could no longer pretend that the past moved in a straight line into the future, so he applied to the Peace Corps. He wanted to get as far away as possible from America.

To West Africa he went, then, after a language course, the relevant jabs, and a course in tropical agriculture. When he first arrived in the village, the children followed him round, chanting jeering French phrases, mindlessly learned from their parents and grandparents, hangovers from the time when the white French had ruled in that part of Africa.

Rick had been in the village for a week when he first played his recorder. One evening he was sitting in the hut which had been given to him, at the edge of the village, and he took out his treble recorder and began playing, just notes, runs, an occasional arpeggio or scale, a kind of getting-to-know-you-again series of sounds. He soon became aware of noises outside his hut, voices whispering agitatedly. He stopped and went to see what was happening. A group of villagers were clustered round the hut, and as Rick emerged one of the elders stepped forward. It transpired that they were all rather angry and worried because they did not like music in their village at night. Why? In case their ancestors were disturbed by the music. Rick immediately apologised, said he had not been told, and that he would not play music again at night. Well, said the elder, they were also worried because they were not sure how their ancestors would feel about white music. The villagers had a very strong sense of hospitality, and said they would ask their ancestors, and then let Rick know what they said.

That night Rick dreamed he was playing his treble by the fire, when his mother and father came towards him out of the flames, took the recorder away from him and threw it on the fire.

The next day the elders came to Rick and said they had asked their ancestors, and the ancestors had said that any music at all at night disturbed them, but they did not mind white music during the day. Rick accepted the judgement and said he would not play music at night again.

The agricultural project progressed; Rick grew lean and strong, at ease with the villagers, respected by them, conversing with them in their language, very occasionally in touch with other Americans, but feeling awkward when called upon to speak English, as if it were a foreign language. The children stopped jeering at him in pidgin French. Sometimes, on holidays he would play his recorders for them, and they would listen or dance. But mostly he played very little. Back in America, the most important time for playing had been in the evening, after the day's work was done, when he was away from other people, when he regained the pleasure of his own company. Now that he could not play after sunset, he would return to his hut at night, take the recorders out of their plastic cases, keep them beside him and put them away when he went to sleep. It was nearly as good as playing. Just looking at the instruments meant he could play anything he wanted to in his head, and he found a kind of contentment in that.

Rick's one-year tour of duty was drawing to a close. Harvests had been reaped, the villagers versed in new, more efficient ways of farming. The village was too remote to be able to benefit from the use of massive machinery, and Rick's presence had served to show how they could make better use of the resources they had. The project was successful, the villagers were grateful, and Rick was beginning to think about leaving. The villagers asked him if he would mind if they prepared a feast for him, a party, a way of saying thank you. Rick was delighted. He had grown very fond of the village and its people and did not want to go. But he knew he could not stay. Meetings were held to discuss how the feast should be organised; they had no ritual which precisely fitted this occasion; they would have to invent and improvise. Much arguing went on late into the night, and Rick smiled as he lay in his hut, feeling great affection for these strangers.

The week leading up to Rick's departure brought a diversion. A herd of rogue elephants had been seen some way away. Messages had come from other villages warning of the animals, their wildness, their fearlessness, their seemingly wanton sense of destructiveness. They had trampled crops, they had attacked children and animals. There was very little the villagers could do except to try and keep a lookout and hope to scare the animals away if they approached. Then there was no word about them, and the village forgot the danger in the excitement of the feast.

On the appointed morning Rick, as the guest of honour, was decked out in flowers, ivory, beads and carvings, all gifts. He apologised for having nothing to give the villagers and they laughed at him and one of them sang a song which listed everything he had taught them, and Rick was delighted. The villagers laughed again. They had all worked and worked on the song and kept it a secret from Rick. It was their main present, they said, one he would not be able to take away with him like an ivory necklace, but one which would stay in his memory. Rick asked them to wait a moment, and then got his recorders. He asked the villagers to sing the song again, and this time he played with them, counterpointing and harmonising and playing his own thank you without words. The villagers applauded, and then sent Rick to rest in the afternoon, in preparation for the feast that evening.

In the centre of the village was a huge fire; meat was roasting, fruits and vegetables were prepared. Everyone brought something, a choice delicacy, a dance, a jump, a kiss from a little child. The village brew was widely drunk, and everything became pleasantly hazy and soft and Rick was both sad and happy, sad to be going, happy to carry the memory with him. For a little while no one noticed a heavy rustle on the outskirts of the village, and then, as the evening wore on, one of the young men came rushing into the centre with the message that the troupe of elephants had been sighted on the edge of the forest. They looked as if they were headed towards the village. No one was quite sure what to do. Because of the revelry, the lookouts had not been so keen at their watch, and the elephants were now very near the village. If the villagers went out to drive them away, there was a danger that the elephants might charge them. Then Rick stood up, a little shaky, and said that he had a suggestion. They were eager to hear. Well, he said, he wanted to play something – partly because he wanted to say thank you again in his own way, partly because he felt he had to. His ancestors were telling him to play. He knew that the villagers' ancesters did not like music at night – but if he made peace and explained that he was leaving – perhaps they would not mind, just this once. The villagers were not sure, but Rick was confident, and this was the Rick they had trusted, the man who had brought new ways to them, which had not harmed them. This was an exceptional time, they thought, so why not.

Rick took his recorders, and playing alternately on the descant and the treble, made an extraordinary music. The village was still. As they listened, all eyes on Rick, sitting by the fire, playing so smoothly so that it sounded like a whole harmony of many instruments, everyone saw two figures emerge from the fire, a man and a woman, in shadow, so that it was impossible to tell who or what they were. The villagers began singing their songs to Rick's melody, and the man and woman took burning branches and carried them away, like bright beacons, down the path which led out of the village.

There was a thunder of sound, like a storm breaking, like a gigantic earthquake, the sound of a herd of elephants in retreat; the sound grew louder and louder, but the villagers sang on and Rick continued to play. The thunder of giant footsteps gradually faded, and with it the singing and the playing faded. Gradually silence took over, a soft, sad, silence, such as no one was used to hearing in a place where there was always sound.

The fire was now very low. In silence everyone dispersed and went to sleep.

In the cold of the early morning, Rick prepared to leave. The villagers clustered round him, saying their final good-byes; one of the lookouts spoke of seeing the elephants many miles away and heading in the opposite direction. A Land Rover was coming to take Rick to the nearest airport, two hundred miles away. Rick walked round the village for the last time. By the grey and black embers of the fire from the night before he found two melted and twisted pieces of plastic, one about the size of a treble recorder, the other the size of a descant recorder. They were cold by now, and he picked them up and put them in his bag. One of the elders was with him and saw him. Do you think I disturbed your ancestors last night, asked Rick. Oh yes, said the elder, I think you did. Music always does disturb them. Didn't you see them come out of the fire?

Yes, I did, said Rick. They reminded me of people I once knew. Of course, said the elder, ancestors always remind you of someone you once knew. I think, added the elder, that you will be glad to get back to a place where you can play music at night.

Perhaps, said Rick. Perhaps.

AFTERWORD

There are various terms for short pieces of prose fiction: 'stories', 'tales', or the one I prefer, which is 'fictions'. Some of the pieces in this book fit into the conventional definition of the 'story' – a short piece of fiction which has a clear beginning, middle and end, and centres round a finite dramatic event. Others are more like stories about a mood, a state of mind, rather than a material happening. Yet others were written to conform to the demands of different media: the drama and publication. These operate in two textual senses: as monologues which can be acted by a performer on stage, radio, and so on, but also as pieces of written text which can be read silently from the page. In these the first-person voice is clearer and more direct, and in each case the idea of some kind of 'audience' (real or imagined for the character) is an implicit presence. The monologue/fictions are 'Whose Greenham', 'I am the Kind of Woman Who', 'Meet My Mother', 'Return to Sender', and 'Nell Gwynne with Cardigan'. The final kind of 'story' in this book is the story that is retold; the taking of a pre-existing text and retelling all of it, or aspects of it, as a way of paying tribute to the way in which one person's fiction can trigger off another's imagination – the way in which myth works. Out of this willing collision of imaginations a new fiction is born. I leave it to the reader to discover the ways in which the themes of motherhood, creativity, possession, dybbuks and music communicate with one another.

Michelene Wandor, London, 1985